space lab

Book One: War of the Noses

Sam Keck

MIKEE BOOKS

Space Lab: War of the Noses

Copyright © 2022 by Sam Keck
ISBN: 978-1-913685-12-6

Published by MIKEE BOOKS
Cover design by designforwriters.com

Disclaimer:

The contents of this book are based on no years of exhaustive academic research in the space and/or science disciplines. Exactly zil facts were harmed, or used, in the making of it. (Official Fact Check Score: 13 and 0/1). Characters aren't anyone you know or have heard about, and are not based on born persons still living or dead, unless by random unlikelihood. In more words:

Space Lab: War of the Noses is an entirely made up thing.

It will not make you cleverer.

now then ...

Discover!

Alien moons inhabited solely by space turds! Amagoo Corporation goons – and goonettes! Escapee lab rats wearing tin foil hats!

All such goodness combining to make this and every future Space Lab adventure one not to be missed. Not if you want your life-force to stop slipping away from you like custard oozing from the crumbly rumbutt of a gingerbread groat.

And I know *I* don't. Want *that*, I mean.

The short version so you can pretend you've read it to the end and got the general gist:

Touching down on Moon B3POBOX77 should be a straightforward space grab for biological samples – worms, bug dust, lichens and other such of nature's treasures. However, unknown to Space Lab's Mission Commander Kubla Khan, and her hated sidekick, Chief Scientific Officer Zander P. Drum, Space Lab isn't the only plunderer of unguarded space bio-resources. Oh, no. There's another bunch of types on the loose in this galaxy, and as luck wouldn't have it, they're a band of stop-at-naught head-pirates from the notorious Earth megacorp, Amagoo.

Add them – the Amagoos – to Space Lab's evolving bionic rat problem, not to mention an alien moon with an intelligent life form closely resembling well-formed stinky turds ... and life for Space Lab's intrepid duo just went from flam to flom.

Oh, and Clone Alpha burns some toast. If that sort of thing butters your crumpet?

THE END.

chapter
one

MISSION COMMANDER KUBLA KHAN, in her fleece-lined khaki gumboots, leapt clumsily onto her workbench, frantically tucking the tails of her white labcoat into the top of her pale pink lucky leggings – the ones with the red lipstick kisses running up and down them.

A rat! Under her bench! A clenching RAT!

She turned up the labcoat's collar and pulled it tightly about her neck, in case one of the furry little boohahas leapt up and went for her jugular. With an audible shiver, she stamped heavily, making regimens of conical flasks on her eye-level shelves jingle like crates of packed-up Christmas bells. She stamped more, sending increasingly panicky, raggedly tuneless chimes across Space Lab's compact Big Research Area laboratory.

Kubla's gaze darted urgently about her feet, her bench, the floor below. Her left hand blindly plucked a large plastic bottle that was hand-labelled Hydrochloric Acid (1%-ish) from her nearest shelf, and held it close to her shoulder, like a shot-putter ready to put.

If there was one thing she hated, she thought, shuddering to the hot molten pit of her stomach, it was Space Lab's infernal plague of –

Before Kubla could finish that thought, the starship's only other natural-born inhabitant came sauntering back from his coffee break, one hand knuckle deep in his grotesquely twisted open mouth, a smallest finger mining for stowaway cookie nuggets in the gaps between his dark-filling'd molars. His other hand was balled up and pressed into a back pocket of his denim jeans, holding them up. And he was, she noted with a curl of her lip, wearing the same catsick-yellow polo shirt with the mayo stain on it, making that a straight forty-four awake days in a row.

Kubla amended her previous thought. If there *was* one thing she hated more than Space Lab's horde of disgusting hairy vermin, it was the useless smear of nematode excrement that held the title of Chief

Scientific Officer: the diminutive, face-fuzzed goblin Zander P. Drum. He was *part* of the hairy vermin horde. One *of* them. The *worst* one.

She'd take rats ahead of him any day of the Voyage. Quest. Thingamajig.

Of her *life*.

Kubla made a mental note, for the nth time, to renew her understanding of the rationality of sending a crew of just two natural-born persons into deep space. The Space Polity Official Document on the matter was 960 pages of psych gunk written by twenty-six authors without a smidge of personality between them. Despite these mind-cloying drawbacks, Kubla found that, when she needed a long ladder up from this particular deep well of despair, the 960 pages were it.

Zander strolled past without seeing her. Relations were that bad. She could have been hanging by the neck from one of the overhead cable lights and he wouldn't have given a flaff.

The twins followed in behind the Chief Scientific Officer. Alpha and Beattie, Space Lab's two general assistance clones – human, but with bits missing – were smiling, as they usually were, without a care in the world. The pair were dressed in identical light-grey tunics and slacks, and had locked arms, in a chummy way, which always reminded Kubla of children in old wars, making jolly while bombs fell and the world around them burned.

She frowned. For reasons she hadn't fully explored, the clones' simplistic happiness always made her want to punch something. She gripped her 1%-ish acid bomb more tightly in her raised fist, and had another episode of hurried glancing about her feet, a strand of her cherry-red hair loosening from her tie-up and falling across her eyes.

'You two,' she commanded curtly, not looking directly at Alpha or Beattie but aware of the shine of their hairless heads as she kept her eyes on where the rat had been.

The clones spoke as one, not perfectly in sync, but teeth-grindingly close.

'Us?' 'Us?'

Kubla sighed. She was being a mean person and she didn't want to be a mean person, because she was *not* a mean person. It was just ... their obedient puppy-dog brown eyes ... she took a quick sweeping look at them ... brown puppy-dog eyes that were somehow irritating the frenkin' *crump* out of her today.

'Yes, *you*,' she said at them, her tone only mildly lightened by force of will, and hardly sweetened at all by a smile that showed way too many teeth. She made eye contact with Alpha, inclining her head as though to ask a favour. 'Drop your schedules, would you? I need you for rat duty.'

Kubla watched the clones check each other's faces, and nod, before turning their attention back to their Mission Commander.

Who was noisily grinding her teeth. You had to tell them everything, exactly as you wanted them to do it. The problem with clones, Kubla thought ... and paused, waiting for a witty new phrase to reveal itself. None did.

'Go get the buckets,' Kubla said robotically, feeling a vein pumping weakly at her temple. 'And the hammers – the soft ones. *Rubber.* Got it?'

'U-hu.' 'U-hu.'

'You will need to go *behind* the petri-dish store. There will be a nest. *Somewhere.* Drag it out. Incinerate *everything*. But not the buckets. Or the hammers this time. Got it?'

'U-hu.' Wider grins breaking out because their replies were perfectly harmonized, a rare but not unknown event and well worth celebrating.

Even Kubla's rat-panic-hardened heart twinged. It *was* kind of cute when that happened. And at least the clones meant it when they smiled. Unlike that home-grown shtump blockage that made up the rest of Space Lab's entire crew.

At least clones didn't do sarcasm, Kubla thought, and her hand plunged into her labcoat pocket for the notepad that wasn't there.

'Oh, crap.'

She wouldn't remember it right. She'd been witty, v. witty, and now she'd forget to remember it correctly, exactly correctly, and it would be gone. *At least clones don't have sarcasm*, she repeated to herself, trying to lock it into memory. *Do* sarcasm? At least clones ... she gave up.

'Crap.'

Zander spoke. 'Kubla, dear?'

She turned on her heel, her gumboots knocking over the plastic tub of fingertip-sized Eppendorf test tubes she'd prepared for sterilizing later that morning. The Chief Scientific Officer, grizzled old short-arse himself, was regarding her from the next bay.

Kubla squinted through her glassware-packed shelves to see him. Blue-capped bottles sparkled under the lab's bright ceiling lights, and Zander's face was distorted by refraction and glimmer into the features of an evil elf. She saw, though, that he was wearing his sneer. The one she had dreamed, more than once, of freezing with liquid nitrogen, and then smashing into a zillion fractured shards with a length of copper pipe.

'*What?*' Kubla spat, then added, 'We've got *rats* in here again. I haven't got time for any of your – your – *whatever it is!*'

'I know all that,' Zander continued, his voice mild and equitable, and not taking his yellowy bloodshot gaze from her.

Kubla seethed, tasted the metallic poison from her fangs, and hissed, '*So what, then?*'

'Just a word of ... advice?' His mouth shrugged, before adding, 'Regarding Pinky and Perky there.' A sideways nod toward the clones. 'About those two,' he added, as if Kubla was some kind of babwrap.

'Advice which *is?*' Kubla bore her eyes into his, ignoring the reflections in glass half blinding her, trying in vain to physically hurt him with the intensity of her hate. She imagined lasers burning into his irises, making his eye jellies smoke and broil and burst out onto his cheeks like ... and caught herself, her thoughts scaring her. Her heart was racing. She breathed out slowly, calming herself.

'So what *is* your advice, Zander,' Kubla asked, diluting her venom a tad.

'My advice,' said Zander, lightly, 'is that you rather

urgently need to tell Pinky and Perky to tell *you* ...' he paused, but went on lowly, almost a whisper, husky, 'what *they* ... can *see*.' And then continuing lightly, 'Because if you don't tell them to, they really won't, y'know.' He shook his head, his contempt for the non-born pair complete.

'Are you just here to – ' Kubla began, her voice rising.

'Pinky, Perky!' Zander abruptly addressed the clones.

'Sir!' 'Sir!'

'Tell Mission Commander Kubla Khan here what you can *see*.'

Kubla swung her gaze to Alpha and Beattie, back to Zander, back to the clones. There was a maddening affiliation between the clones and Zander, despite his constant mocking of them. She was knowingly jealous of it.

'U-hu-hu,' the clones affirmed to Zander, before turning back to Kubla, hands behind backs.

'Missssionnn Commanander Khhan,' they began sweetly, enjoying themselves. 'Th-there iss a Rat-rat. A-A grea-at b-igg onne. Itt isis runrunning ing downn ththe hanngginng li-ight ca-able and and ...'

Kubla snapped her face upwards so fast a cord in her

neck twanged painfully. In startling close-up, the dankest, foulest, horriblest shit-brown fur-foe filled her view. She heard her crazed, throaty scream quickly reach the back wall of Space Lab's compact Big Research Area laboratory and bounce back, just as the rat emitted its own ululating battle squeal.

Kubla flinched as the thing landed on her head, its unimaginably gruesome scratchy claws skidding and scrambling in her hair. Her hair! A pallid, faintly warm tail lay idly for a second across her nose, trailed over her forehead as the bubonic buttslitherer's weight shifted madly, like a mad thing, a thing possessed, with a hellish purpose.

Her face a twisted mask of waxy horror, her whole body gyrating disco style, Kubla threw her free hand at it, miraculously actually grabbed it, and dug her long pink nails into it.

'*Got* you, you [erased from the record for reasons of profanity] piece of [erased: ditto]! I'm gonna [erased from the record for reasons of common decency] and [erased from the record in accord with International Space Exploration Act 27 iii (b) Section 1007 X]!!!'

The rodent, as if understanding Kubla entirely, and if so, rightly offended by her inconsiderate words of personal insult, clamped two pairs of opposing scalpel-sharp incisors – its pokey old rat teeth, in other words – onto the hard gristle curl of her ear. And started to crunch.

Had the clones not averted their gaze to protect their delicate young brains, they might have informed Kubla that the rat was an unusually large one – a record-breaker about the size of a fully grown late 21st Century Hunting Chihuahuahua. And that it was, rather unusually, wearing headgear consisting of a scrunched tin foil hat encrusted here and there with two-millimetre nanochip control boards, and held on to its head by a chin strap made of red plastic-coated wire.

Funny, that.

chapter
two

THE HUNTING CHIHUAHUAHUA, along with
the Elgin Marboolets, and the Stinging Postman, are
examples of late 21st Century *Uphes*, or, as Professors in
buttoned-up cardies call them: 'Ultra-Phenomena'.

*Aunt Annie's Complete Dictionary of Known Words
(and Things), free edition,* describes it thusly:

Uphe n. (yoo-fay; or, Northern: Uffie) slang

*A thing that everyone seems to know about without
knowing how they know or who told them, or why.*

*Further examples include: Gants, Crynoisettes,
Flockstupper Barbstarbs, Leg Booms, Babwraps and
Moops. And Floonts.*

chapter
three

KUBLA ENCOURAGED her eyelids to remain closed. Would happily have had them pegged.

Still pleasantly drugged out, she was enjoying the white noise of Space Lab's infirmary, which reminded her quite clearly of the ocean. She had also been more than enjoying, while resting, a spectacularly successful box-set of personal memory recall meditations, known to Kubla's mind voice as MRMs.

And MRMs were a hundred and ninety six percent *zoot*.

Kubla, attempting to not be really awake, wanted her MRMs to continue for as long as she could summon them – forever not being too long a time-frame. And so, with a relaxing, piggish snore, she let another roll its lazy way in:

Her Grandfather Khan, whom Kubla knew only as a crotchety but mostly kind-meaning old coffin dodger (his words, not hers) had wound down his days at his shore-front property on Long Island, U.S.A, stargazing, fixing up an old sailboat, and playing, through warm afternoons, the cinefilms of his childhood. There he was now, sitting, staring, in the loft of a half-derelict building he still referred to as Hitler's Folly, his own celluloidal recalls leaving him agog at his youth, and the simpler world he'd lived through.

'Un-believable,' he spoke to little girl Kubla, mouth open in a pout, Cuban cigar hovering nearby like a UFO returning to its mothership. His other hand bunching up in his scraggy old paisley pattern dressing gown, very like a child grasping its comforter.

Kubla's mind effortlessly replayed her grandfather's films again now, as she had many times as both older child and adult. Flickery images on a white sheet pinned with bent nails to a bare wood wall of the falling down (allegedly U-boat torpedoed) old boathouse. A breeze bringing inside the salty smells of late afternoon, promising a cool evening, and ruffling up the flimsy screen, which was showing ...

a slip of a lad, a willow wand, dives into a swimming hole, swims away, treads water, climbs out onto a distant rock, a huge smile for the camera operator. Now he's chasing his dog, Rancho, until the wolfhound concedes defeat, and will run no more, but can still gain sway by lathering the boy's face with a tongue red as a pepper – and a furious wagging of tail. Cut to: a shyly received birthday song, bright slices of cake, squares of chocolate brownie. Her boy-grandfather's guilty side-look, too old for praise now, or gifts, or an arm across his shoulder.

Kubla saw plainly her Grandfather Khan's face as he watched his youth pass by. He wore an unbelieving, lips-parted smile, his old hands now folded into his skinny armpits, cigar held tightly between his teeth, his vintage Sony Walkman headset like an white-orange torc around his neck.

His life defined by the freedom of music anywhere, attached to the hip; his granddaughter's here, a frillion miles away in a starship infirmary that had the aroma of … was that burning?

Becoming more alert now, Kubla, with a strong will, pressed her eyelids together, needing more balm to soothe her recently traumatized self. It was something she'd always done, when a harsh parental word or barbed schoolyard jibe was sent her way, cut deeply into her. She'd enclosed, away from the world outside, her Self.

And then *restored* her Kublaself, afterwards.

If ever the *real* best memory recalls ran down, or were deemed by her torched mind insufficient for the damage received, it was no problem, because she'd learned to make up new ones, either fictional in their entirety – coloured unicorns not being uncommon, and talking flowerpots – or else, also fun, creative embellishments of actual real events, altered by her storyteller's craft so that she, Kubla, didn't flounder, but came out on top, and winning.

This she did now, suddenly seeing herself sitting proudly on a television studio chair, at a discussion desk. A woman of vibrancy. Her eyes as clearly defined and radiant as the Shamrock projected onto a backdrop screen behind her, to honour St Patrick.

Kubla watched her glossed lips smile and move, move as they smiled. She was: Amazing. And she was, amazingly, saying the words '21st Century Ultra-Phenomena' on Channel 45 News, this only weeks before Space Lab's launch from Hebridean Space Port.

She'd worn her green dress, the one that fanned out from the waist and yet suited her bold height, made something of it, drew attention to her shoulders, her strong neck. Her face had been a glowing sensation of makeover wizardly – her hair set just so – and she'd *owned* it.

Her interview on the daytime feed had immediately followed the rolling headline story, which came fresh from that morning's unusually newsworthy manhunt, wherein a police sniffer dog, named Sniffer, had expertly tracked down a fleeing burglary suspect by wit of the poor fellow's uncontrollable farts. Such treacherous bodily give-aways described by a group of passerby earwitnesses as being uncannily *miaow-like* in tone.

Sniffer, a NewsReal official Hero of the Day, was to be seen on loop receiving a home-made Ribbon of Valour from a smiley old lady nobody knew about, and then wolfing down a specially made vegan doggy cake from Megan's For Vegans, the downtown store from where the crime spree had originated, the culprit being a recent Customer of the Month, and, according to the arresting officer, possibly dangerously B-12 deficient.

'I've seen this kind of thing before,' the officer commented directly to camera, adding after some extensive ruffling of floppy dog ears and, from the cake-faced Sniffer, an accompanying whine of pleasure: 'We need to, as a community, be more extra-vigil.'

Kubla, ever the ingenious whizz, cleverly made reference to the story in her own replies.

Space Lab, she suggested to camera – at the time she'd imagined addressing the world's population, young children cross-legged on rugs before television walls, parents in their autocars, olds in their roving Hives – would be just like, in fact almost exactly alike to, that hero police dog. Roaming the universe, *sniffing out* – she emphasized those words by first widening her eyes, then drawing down a cheeky conspiratorial wink – all sorts of, not baddies as such, but *goodies*.

'Space Lab really is and should be considered a 21st Century Ultra-Phenomena,' Kubla finished, triumphant.

'Oh wow!' the newscaster glittered, overly impressed by the cleverness of Kubla's link, and also at the first person she'd heard say the unabbreviated 'Ultra-Phenomena' since she was nine. 'You will literally be ... sniffing out Space Farts?' She waved a hand, conjured her own creative ephemera. 'You'll be like ... a Hunting Chihuahuahua ... *but in Space*!'

'Well ...' Kubla, a natural born people-pleaser, at first agreed: 'Yes.' Then added, with pride in herself, a contradictory, 'a-and No. Space Lab is, in fact, actually equipped with the latest post-web technologies, and is capable of *sniffing out* biological as well as inanimate materials. We will be searching for, collecting, and bringing home a whole galaxy of resources. For the benefit of people kind, and so on and so forth like that really.'

It was a triumph. Smart *and* sassy.

The newscaster's perfectly immobile face told the world she hadn't listened to a word Kubla had just said. 'And farts, right?' she beamed and blinked.

'Well,' Kubla, deflated a little, 'technically ... I suppose ... yes.'

'And there you have it!' As the camera left Kubla, and an aide beckoned for her to quietly leave the set. 'Here on Channel 45 News, where we put the Real into NewsReal. Space Lab Mission Commander Kubra Khan, going nobly, like a space hound, into space, to seek – and *sniff!* – the farts this planet needs. Now, let's hope it's not farting out there right now – here's Justin with the Weather.'

Kubla, feeling half a lifetime distant from that small embarrassment, lay flat on a dolly under dimmed infirmary lamps, and let loose a stringy bubble of spit, which she absentmindedly sucked back in. She settled her head into her soft pillow, her mind now monologuing pleasantly.

The Hunting Chihuahuahua – or, to give it its real name – the Hun T'ing Chihuahuahua, Kubla lectured to herself, was a completely made up thing. As were several of the most prominent Uphes.

Kubla was entirely behind the notion of completely made up 21st Century Ultra-Phenomena, if for one reason only: they had finally given artists something to draw that people actually wanted to see. No more whatever-that-was-supposed-to-be, please and thank you very much, Kubla almost spoke, her lips moving slugily.

Other completely made up Uphe's that late 21st Century persons adored mentioning to each other in conversation, or seeing on walls, Kubla continued, with a finely educated air, included three of everyone's absolute favourites: Cheese Men, Egg-Ligs, and Gants, which were like ants, but with tiny coats on.

When it came to *serious* Uphe status, however, intoned Kubla as she skilfully rounded up, the Hun T'ing Chihuahuahua always took the biscuit – and suddenly realizing she might have made a bit of a joke, her hand felt for her notepad, and when it wasn't there, she opened her eyes.

A cool blue light was flashing. And she definitely smelled burning.

'Oh, crap.'

She tried to sit up and failed as black smoke spread in unfurling ribbons across the ceiling above her. Her cheeks felt the glow of heat. And then a sudden irresistible wave of druggy sleepiness sent her eyes rolling backwards, her mind struggling futilely in a frothy whiteout as her head hit the pillow.

'Oh ... crap.'

chapter
four

<u>Observations of a Large Brown Rat in a Tin Foil Hat</u>
(Translation from the brainstem, as recorded by
resonant frequency fluctuations sideloaded to *Aunt
Annie's Complete Dictionary of Known Words (and
Things), free edition.)*

...... she leave with Slave A to hospical then sharp on
arm make sleepy like.

Master him put face upwards like it had sniff
something bad, and roll eyes in. Him Master look at
Slave B and make eyes smaller and make black face fur
shook like bristles, bad, bad.

Him Master point about with finger like poke. Him lips move. Him show teeth make bad noise.

Slave B then dids takes eleven green papers it clean spatters of red blood from around. Around is the high up, the shining on the above, the sit on, the floor ground.

Slave B give red blood eleven green paper in waste disposal flapper, where, hee hee, rats wait and drag away behind walls and through dark home hee hee.

Him Master point and poke. New green paper clean spot, put in waste disposal flapper for rats.

Him Master hung face down and walk with hands on knees. Point and poke. New green paper clean spot, put in waste disposal flapper for rats.

Him Master leave face down and only eyes move. Then Him stand and look up, down, over here and take something from wears and rub thumb on and us feel need for pee but not here so leave.

Pee pee pee pee pee! Wheeee! <<End of Translation>>

chapter
five

KUBLA'S NECK FELT GOOEY, and there was a dull pain on the left side of her head – with her fingers she found a thick mass of bandage there, about the size and shape of a deep-sided cereal bowl, that entirely cupped her ear.

'Really?' she asked Alpha, her mind clear as Spring. 'Was the damage ... *that* bad?'

'Suits you, Ma'am!' came the clone's cheerful reply.

He was standing over by the toast machine, warming his hands and face in the hot steam rising from it. Beside him on the Recovery Room's bijou kitchenette worktop there stood, Jenga-style, a stack of blackly charred toaster rejects reaching almost halfway to the ceiling, so impossibly balanced that surely only the scorched tower's uncanny beauty was holding it up.

On the ceiling above, both the smoke alarm and emergency light casings were smashed open. A long-handled broom lay across the floor, with the broom's plastic bristles melted into the shape of an immaculately coiffured quiff. Fire extinguisher foam was dappled liberally about the grey walls and ceiling.

Kubla put two and two together. She didn't have to be Sherlock Jones to work out what had happened while she was dozing – unsupervised use of the toaster being only the start of it.

A few short, sharp rebukes came to mind, but she decided against. Don't bark at the clone who feeds you, she thought, and reached, again, for where her notebook was usually to be found. She sighed. Where had it gotten to?

'Toast on its way, Ma'am.' Clone Alpha said, as chipper as a British butler with a full day of service ahead of him.

Kubla sucked sweet toasty air in through her nose, eager for her post-procedural snack – her insides starting to gurgle – and she sneezed.

'R'member,' she commanded – her voice was softened to a purr by the dag end of the anaesthetics, but still carried authority – 'I want mine brown all over, but not black. Black toast isn't good, so not that. Brown all over, like I said. And leave it to steam off, for a minute. And then scrape on as much butter as it will hold.' Her stomach bubbled its agreement loudly. 'Please,' she added, belatedly.

She watched Alpha do as he'd been told, and bring the toast on its grey plastic plate to her on the infirmary bed, which had been set to a sitting position. She took the goodies in hand, eagerly chose a slice, and slowly bit down, moaning orgastically as she did so.

Alpha immediately turned his attention to the vital signs monitors fixed to the wall beside the bed, but Kubla patted his arm. 'No, no,' she said 'it's just me enjoying my naughty toast.'

She grinned and winked at him, taking a larger bite, before, with a shrug, folding the rest of the butter-sodden slice into her mouth, using both hands, pushing with fingers, the way she'd done as a child. The sensation of salty pleasure as she chewed and swallowed was almost too much to bear.

'Sorry,' she spoke with her mouth half-full, 'I'm disgusting but … I needed that.'

She took a sip of the wrong tea Clone Alpha had already brewed, and began to nibble her second slice.

The recovery from accident or illness was something Kubla had always fully invested in. It was ... she made up a new word for it ... *floom.*

Her mouth curled downwards. She touched the cereal bowl bandage again, and grimaced. Not from pain – Alpha had been more than generous with the analgesics – but from the memory. And not, even, from recall of the rat, which horror she'd already buried in some deep, dark vault never to see the light of life. No, the curl of her mouth was for the memory, sharp and clear, of Zander P. Drum, and his role in the affair.

Why hadn't he told her the rat was there? Hollered a warning? Whacked at it, or something?

Because he hated her. That was the only possible conclusion. He hated her *as much as she hated him.*

The thought stunned her. That his intensity of hate should match hers ... she shivered, and Clone Alpha unfolded a fresh white cellular blanket and draped it across her shoulders.

'Thank you, Alpha,' she said, grateful for it. 'You take good care of me.'

Unlike, she obsessed, her mission partner, who'd left her to face abomination while standing idly by ... and, presumably, *enjoying* it.

'I don't actually know where it went wrong with

Zander,' she confided, lightly so as not to reveal the extent of her hurt. Alpha cocked his head a little to show that he was apparently listening. 'I mean, it seemed okay, *pre-flight*. We had the compatibility workshop in Palm Springs. And Zander was – *fine*. It was *good*.'

'U-hu,' from Alpha, on autopilot.

'I mean, he slept. A lot.' She chuckled. 'And I had to put the handouts from the workshops he'd missed through his door and all. But he seemed good with that. Then there was the thing with the police, and him losing his shoes. Which would be upsetting for anybody. I mean, your *shoes*, Alpha!'

Kubla leaned over the edge of the infirmary bed and regarded Alpha's footwear, light-grey canvas tie-ups that she remembered choosing herself from a glossy SciTech catalogue at some purchasing meeting or other, before she'd ever dreamed of being one of Space Lab's crew, what seemed like decades ago, and decided not to try to explain. The clone's shoes were chosen *for* him, and for no other reason than to match exactly the colour of walls, floors and ceilings. Whereas – Kubla gulped loudly at the thought – if anyone had stolen shoes of hers, ones she had carefully bought, worn and *inhabited*, she'd have felt ... violated.

'Anyway, the point is, Zander and me were good, *pre-launch*. And when we woke up for first planetfall, we were good then too. I remember we were.'

Their first suspended animation had lasted a mind-warping ninety-four years, which of course felt like you'd just closed your eyes for a second during *Murder She Wrote* and then for some reason snapped awake feeling yeugh.

Foetal helplessness, the pamphlets she'd read called it. And they weren't, those glossy phlets, in her opinion, far off being exactly right.

The immediate new-born baby need, once the restroom had been visited, was for human to human interaction, of any kind. And so for Kubla to find the still barely known Zander already there in the Watsit Room (as they'd soon began to call it) ... it was as welcome, to see him, nearly as much as an English Muffin would have been, with a personal pot of Yorkshire Tea beside it. A treat she wasn't allowed on waking, and so of course doubly craved, her intestines tunefully imploring of her 'Why?' and 'Whyyyyyy?' over and over, in increasingly embarrassing volumes as she walked in.

Zander, standing over by the tartan coffee table, was slowly bending, as carefully as a citizen thinking back a while to his hundredth birthday, the aim being to dock his butt without incident into the comfy comfort of a paisley pattern armchair, one of a pair with the coffee table between them.

And, she thought, he had the oddest hair. It looked – and appeared to steam even – like a warmed-up horse flump. Which had amused Kubla, a man looking like that, vulnerable. Had he not checked himself in the restroom mirror? Her amusement, she remembered now as she sipped her cooling tea, being quickly drowned by another, powerful wave of strange feeling – that she was just so pleased to see him.

There wasn't anything major squirmy between them – they were comrades on this mission, and it was as comrades they'd behaved. But there had been something. More than nothing. From her to him, and him to her. She was sure of it.

Kubla had opened the conversation, her voice shaky, feeling tentative, like her tubes had shrunk. 'Can I ask a personal question?' And not waiting for an answer, and before her tummy got another whine in: 'Is your pee black?'

'Textbook,' the wan-faced Zander growled back, in a self-deprecating tone she liked, and showing her his gums in a smile – gums like pale plaster above yellowed porcelain teeth. 'Here, let me get you a frothy cap.' He crossed slowly to the wall vendor on wobbly legs. 'It'll take away the taste in your mouth of, what would you call it?'

'Phlegm?' suggested Kubla. 'Moose?'

'Moose phlegm,' Zander had agreed, nodding, his lips tight in a pleasant, boyish, but slightly pained smile.

The vendor made her a bubble-topped cappuccino in a paper cup hardly bigger than a thimble. When Zander handed it to her, his hands were noticeably shaking, as were hers receiving it.

'How long til we're over this?' she'd asked, though she knew the answer: forty-eight hours. That's how long it took for a full system flush. Meanwhile they were supposed to drink electrolytes only, but Kubla didn't want to be prissy, to ruin the vibe between them.

'Lug that and you'll be fine,' Zander had said. So she'd done so.

The warmth, the smooth bite of it, bolting down her gullet to her empty stomach and beyond ... it was inexplicably *cosy*. Just what she'd needed.

'Thanks!' she'd even said, overdoing it, but what the frunk? There was a thing called social responsibility, and she knew all about that, was part of her job description really when you thought about it.

She'd shat then for two days, hourly. Could have managed to direct it through the eye of a needle, had such a trick been demanded of her.

And not until this moment did she realize ...

Kubla found her notebook down by her right knee, extracted the pen it neatly housed, and wrote on a fresh page, pressing the nib down hard:

Z laced my frekkin' cappuccino.

Then she folded the notebook and held it in her fist.

'Tell you what,' she told Clone Alpha, coldly, and when he dutifully cocked his head: 'You and me are going to *get* that excuse for a person. And we're going to *get him good.*'

chapter
six

SHOULD A LONELY FLY, wide of eye and deft of wing, wander the stale, windless air of Space Lab's grey curving corridors, looking for action, and land inconspicuously on an unadorned wall in the most appetizingly odoriferous of the two born persons living quarters, *what would it see?*

It would see Zander P. Drum, his bulldog's bum mouth twisted tight as a pickpocket's purse, and subtly twitching while, with a watchmaker's dexterity, and perched toward the front edge of a blue-and-white striped deck-chair, this half-naked Rumpelstiltskin used the thick fingers and thumbs of both hands to weave a fine copper wire neatly and carefully behind his left foot's pinky toenail.

Of which toenails ... the fly, without the capacity to shade its gaze with the hurried blink of an eyelid or two, must endure mercilessly.

Think for these toenails: torn apart shrapnel shards. In colour? Bio-luminescent orange. Texture of nail surface? Sticky.

Just the mere thought of landing, softly, and gently locking its proboscis onto a toenail's candyfloss fungal surface ... our fly shivers its delicate wings, rubs its front bits together in delightful eagerness, and so in its exquisite anticipation dies, falling unnoticed to the floor, at best a rat snack, at worst never having existed at all.

Propped on a toolbox, and illuminated brightly from beneath, the in-betweens of Zander's toes offered (our fly'd have observed, were it not just dispensed with) a cheeseboard of mulchy yellows, curdy whites, and viral bluey greens. Though, all things considered, it was the dayglo orange fungus toenail horrors that really cut the mustard.

Maintaining his perch as close as he dared to the folding deck-chair's edge, his under-toned tummy muscles straining, Zander continued single-mindedly with his task, stringing wire from toe to toe, undernail to undernail, until his left foot held aloft a five-propped copper line that twinkled in the glow of his portable Tilly lamp like fairy grotto lights.

Zander quickly wound the ends of wire about a nearby battery cell's voltage terminals, and, with a grunt of pleasant surprise, settled his aching back into the bumper XXXL cushion that awaited it.

Clone Beattie watched from a corner, standing proud as a midwife, her hands clasped one in the other.

Zander's relaxing body produced a sigh, while with half-lidded pupils he regarded his left foot, his lips untwisting into a dreamy smile.

'So how about that?' he breathed in wonder. 'It only darn works, sure it does.'

He rubbed his fingers slowly on his jeans, sniffed each digit, then put both hands behind his head, his fingertips digging through his thick, unwashed locks.

'This calls for a can of,' he told the clone.

Beattie turned on her heel, pressed buttons on the wall vendor, and moments later brought Zander a filled paper cup.

Zander quaffed it. Grimaced.

'Sorry, Sir.' Beattie taking the empty cup from him. 'You were due your vitamins, and I thought – '

'You thought you'd poison me where I sit with that poop? Nah, forget it – I get it.' Zander gave Beattie a generous wink. 'Respect to you, Dobbie,' he said, good-humouredly, watching her dutifully recycle the cup through the waste disposal flap.

'Now,' said Zander, lightly, 'that I'm comfy and under the care of my new tootsie spa, let's have at business.'

He picked up a palm-held, rolled the thumb cursor, and turned his head to watch a large brown rat emerge somewhat reluctantly from under the room's single bunk, as if it had been called from important business.

The rat, rather unusually, was wearing headgear, consisting of a scrunched tin foil helmet encrusted here and there with two-millimetre nanochip control boards, and held on to the rat's head by a chin strap made of red plastic-coated wire.

Zander thumbled the cursor again and the suddenly rejuvenated rodent scurried to the wall vendor, hopping expertly over Beattie's feet as it went.

Zander and Beattie – who'd given it room – watched the rat scale a pre-made string ladder to the control panel, press a button with its nose, and wait patiently as, before its twitching whiskers, a paper cup was filled to the brim with sweet-smelling and delightfully pink popcorn.

It glanced over its shoulder at Zander, who gave it

two thumbs from behind his head, and a nod. And so, returning its attention to the task, and finding enough space around the cup to make a comfortable perch to sit back on two legs and use its front pair like hands, the rat rather delicately nibbled a puffed kernel.

'Go for it, Winston,' from Zander. 'Why not? Hard work should always pay off.'

The rat took a moment to clean its whiskers, then grabbed the top of the paper cup in its jaws, and, retreating down the ladder, immediately tipped half the contents on the floor.

Another glance at Zander.

'Nah, don't apologize,' said Space Lab's Chief Scientific Officer, warmly. 'You did good today, wee fella. Genius.'

He thumbled again, and the rat headed home, dragging its half-empty cup of sweet reward and pausing only to consider Zander's wired foot, from which the smell of heated-up mildew was rising. The rodent's nose twitched upwards, a master chef savouring a well-seasoned soup.

'Judge all you like, chum!' Zander encouraged it. Then added: 'Between your gang and Mrs Jeeves over there, you keep me going. You really do, you two.'

The rat now seeming unsure whether to stay or go.

'You're my angels,' Zander spoke with affection. 'I love ya both and equally. And as for that numpty you two set up for a fall this afternoon ... you naughty wee scallywags, you!'

Beattie blushed as pink, and as sugar-sweet, as the popcorn she was sweeping up with a small pan and brush. She gave out a giggle.

'You went too far though, you know that?' Zander's tone was more admonishing than he'd planned, but he pressed on. 'I shouldn't have listened to you. Should have kept well clear of your shenanigans. You *used* me.'

He held the palm-held up to his eyes, and shook his head in regret. He'd had control of the rat, and ran the affair hands – and palm-held – in pockets. But when the helper clones and vermin were *devising* operations ...

Ah, what the hell. What was done was done.

'Away with you both,' he said, and the rat headed sulkily for under the bed, still dragging its cup.

'I'm going to have to pay for your handiwork someday,' Zander called after it, and after Beattie, who'd palmed the door and was leaving. 'Do you realize that? From now on, the numpty's gonna hate the skin I'm in, so she is.'

'She already did!' Beattie shot over her shoulder.

'Just plain *evil*, you are,' Zander told her, with a growl and a shake of his grisly head, and a 'Tsk!', and then an 'Oooo-aa-aaah!' as the toenails on his left foot began to glow, spark and erupt into purple flame, and his deck-chair collapsed beneath him.

chapter
seven

SPACE LAB'S auto-manoeuvre was sensed by her crew in ways subtle, personal and with an oddity they were learning to get used to, this far from the normality of Earth.

Zander, fire extinguisher still in hand, felt his bowels move, downwards and to the left.

Beattie, who'd been batting at singed toenails with a fire blanket, felt her tongue tingle, brightened, then, suddenly remembering it was her turn to stay home, turned the edges of her mouth downwards.

'Ah you, you'll still have fun, I know you will,' was Zander's consolation.

Kubla meanwhile, striding from the sick bay ahead of her attendant clone, had a strong sense of *déjà vu*.

A sense – if sense it was – she, by the way, ranked one step lower than Floont Fancying in the league table of human emotional weirdnesses. To be blunt, she hated it, and her stride increased as if she hoped to quickly overtake it.

Oh, it *sounded* cool ... and *French* ... but there could be no pleasure in it, and she took none, not a bit. For Kubla, *déjà vu* was merely a falsehood, a useless premonition, a fraud. Trying to deceive her into thinking that something embarrassing was about to happen to her. Had *already* happened to her, in her immediate future.

Of course it would be an embarrassment. There was no question it wouldn't be, that thing coming.

The sensation then was ... a rippling back in time ... warning her ... so that she could do ... what? Avoid it? No. Prepare herself? No!

It was a nothing. A non-thing, she thought. And yet it had to be shared, always, with another person. *That* was its only peculiar power.

'I've got a feeling of déjà vu,' Kubla told Clone Alpha, unable to stop herself. 'But I don't want to talk about it.'

The dull grey corridor curved leftwards towards the

Big Research Area laboratory. Kubla's mind, ramped up to full *vu*-inspired annoyance, despite her dismissiveness, bulged ahead as if to extend around the corner and see the fate that lay there. Another bionic rat to undermine her authority? Or was Corridor 1 about to crumple under pressure loss, twist about her, so that she was crushed within a metal tube, her body mangled, soon to be extruded into space through tears torn in Space Lab's titanium outer husk, as the ship silently disintegrated – and somehow she was supposed to feel embarrassed about it?

Well, as it happens, surprise surprise, neither. And nothing.

In any case, Kubla's left boot wasn't fitting well. She paused to stamp it on more securely, and the unsettling sensation was forgotten forever.

Clone Alpha felt the Space Lab manoeuvre for what it was. Oh, the ship has just slowed, preparatory to planetfall. Wheee!

'My turn to ride in the lander,' he informed Kubla, who didn't bother to reply.

'Hurry up, you pair!' Zander's bark arrived from up ahead. 'I need to lay some rapid space cable. That means we're *on*. Give me five – no, better make it two.'

As they reached him, Zander pummelled a pressure pad on a door labelled Refreshment Room 2, and stepped inside with a small, and possibly unconscious, waggle of his butt.

Clone Beattie greeted Alpha by taking his hand.

'Right, clones,' commanded Kubla, walking on hastily. 'If our ... Chief Engineer is right and time is limited, we ought to make straight for the lander. Initiate procedure 7P. And check our itinerary, but if I'm not mistaken, this will be B3POBOX77 – our first *moon*!'

Kubla felt some pleasant spine-fizz – Moon B3POBOX77 was high on the list of planetary bodies likely to be inhabited by multicellular life forms. She was excited!

Her fingers touched the breakfast bowl bandage covering her left ear. 'Gosh, I hope this isn't going to be uncomfortable in the Skinz.'

'It suits you,' commented Beattie from behind her, and, for just a moment, Kubla was sure she detected the slightest, far-off echo of sarcasm from the clone who would command Space Lab in their absence. Sarcasm? From a *clone*? Kubla dismissed it. Surely not. Absolutely. Not.

Pausing to let the clones get ahead of her – and to

scrutinize their blank faces – Kubla heard a violent vacuum-suck scream from a bathroom air conditioning unit that sounded like it had gone to check out one too many horror movie cellars. She hurried on, Zander speaking from behind her as he hastened to catch her up.

'If you need to go too, I'd choose another location,' he suggested.

Kubla walked briskly, aware he was following closely behind her, too closely.

'Seriously,' Zander confided. 'Go before we go, though. Just ... not in there. It needs five. Or ten. Oh, make it fifteen. Years?'

And as they neared the lander prep room, 'I'm actually being nice now,' he continued. 'You need to fly empty. And it's the rules, actually. To do with weight, I presume? And there being no potties in space, as a general rule.'

Kubla decided she ought to reply. They'd be spending the next many hours as a close-knit team exploring space for the benefit of Earth, and had to work together, no matter what. So she swallowed her bile, mentally waved a white flag about, and turned to address her enemy professionally.

'Thank you for your informative help,' she said,

with what she called her winning smile. 'And also your concern. But don't worry about me, I'll be perfectly fine.'

chapter
eight

A Note Of

THE TOILET BEHAVIOURS ENJOYED by off-Earth explorers have oddly fascinated people with too much time to think about stuff since the dawn of science fiction, through to the present day goings on up there.

Something to do with tubes and sucking it out; and, would that be something I'd like to do / I should do / I'm missing out on in my daily life, etc. etc. etc.

Readers of such an unsatisfied nature are referred by the author herein, to another title in the Space Literary genre, for a complete understanding of all anybody needs to know:

How Little Space-Bears Go Pee-pee and Poop – a lift the flap book in 50 words by L. Rantzenburger Krubb, published 2038 by SpaceBear Books, Inc., 114 Upper Goat Lane, Norwich, U.K.

'INITIATE COUNTDOWN PLEASE.'

Kubla watched Zander's gloved hand, on her command, begin tapping the edge of the lander's control console and, as he muttered his ten, nine, eight routine, she felt butterflies tickle up and down her insides and race along her arms.

'Green for Go,' Zander grunted, and with the slightest of flutters in her palms, and the first 'I'm full, don't jiggle me!' notice from her bladder, she knew Big Lander was free from Space Lab, had become a tiny, helpless thing, floating in space. With a tiny, helpless crew inside it, she imagined.

Kubla drew in a deep breath that seemed to stop before it should have. She thought deliberately: Zander knows what he's doing. And then: the selfish groat wouldn't be here if he didn't. So be …… Calmness.

They descended without talking, Kubla watching the green monitors to the left and right of Zander, who sat in the front seat like her father had in their family car, crouched as if someone had just sucker punched him in the woowads. So far the screens were showing zilch, and Kubla, who was directly behind her Chief Scientific Officer, found her attention drawn to the back and top of his head, and a loose thread in the otherwise perfectly tight stitching of his Skinz fire-safety balaclava that stuck up like, she thought, one of those hairs that grow where they shouldn't, midway between the eyebrows being a favourite location, or corkscrewing crazily from an otherwise pristinely hairless region of ear, or nose, or down there even. She felt a strong urge to reach forward and pluck it out, and resisted with an equally powerful force of will.

She touched the left side of her own balaclava instead, gingerly, feeling the bandage protruding there, and beneath it, her throbbing and quite hot ear.

Clone Alpha was to her left, Clone Beattie's empty seat to her right. They were a team of planetary explorers. Earth's first. And their privileged asses were about to write another page of human history.

Minutes falling. A brown planetary body emerging on the right screen, and growing to fill it.

And then they were off, rollercoastering through Moon B3POBOX77's light atmosphere to the soundtrack of whining metal. She was used to this now, though; it was only reassurance that all was alright, still.

They were experienced players, Kubla told herself. They were *it*. And continued with positive thoughts while she willed herself not to sick up a butter toast surprise, or give in to the pressure building inside her aching bladder. How long could she hold it ... ? The thought of letting go through both ends here and now ... unthinkable. If sadly not entirely unprecedented.

Electrostatic flashes on green monitors; earthquake rumbles under her seat growing to the levels of a threat, before slowly giving way, fading to a memory, as Zander touched down without even the tiniest of bumps.

'Sorry 'bout that folks.' Big Lander's pilot sounding mightily impressed with his own flying.

At the sound of Clone Alpha clapping, Kubla permitted herself to join in. Give the repellent gnu-gnu his due, he was an ace flyer. A buttmaggot of a human, but an ace flyer.

And possibly because she'd clapped, she later thought, when they'd helmeted and open-hatched and she'd made sure Clone Alpha had ticked off the procedure sheet, Zander broke rank and stood aside, with a jester's flourish of his arm, to let her lead them down the ladder – a first.

Kubla wasn't going to waste the opportunity.

'This is one small step,' she said, swiftly cocking a leg onto the ladder's first rung, hearing the mounting excitement, the sheer incredible wowsyness in her voice. 'One small itzy step ...' and then taking a few more steps down the ladder, holding on with her monkey grips tightly, '... for humanity ...' she gulped, emotional, halfway down, adding through her thickening throat, 'One really, really, REALLY big step for woman ... and me!'

Zander's boot pressing on her two hands causing her to let go of the ladder, hearing in her panic his amused, 'Hey now, Willa! No need to hop!'

Kubla, momentarily mid-air, could do little but float slowly down, to land two-footed on the moon surface. She did, however, cushion herself with a slight bend of the knees, and then stand tall amid the twin tiny mushrooms of pumicey dust cloud her boots had set in motion.

She sighed happily. Her gymnastics coach, Ma

K'eene, would have shat rosettes, seeing that, from her, Kubla, bottom of the class always.

'Mission log,' Kubla said breathily, but as cool as you like, hands on her hips as she surveyed. 'Moon strata yielding with particulate covering; medium to firm foothold. Going good. Advise rest of crew: low grav as expected, estimate one ish?'

'Girl,' from Zander, loudly in her right ear, and sounding more than impressed. 'You're a leg-end!' And then directed up to their clone, 'I'm both feet down on this pie crust too, now — you following Smeagol?'

At which moment Kubla took another small step and immediately doubled over, eyes streaming, throat gagging, *dying*.

'*Smell* ...' she croaked – her last word helping others, such was the person she was, her mind noted.

'You, okay?' from Zander, before it hit him too. 'Oh, what the ...? *NO!*'

He staggered into her, his arms windmilling as he struggled to keep his balance in the unfamiliar gravity, bellowing: 'No, no, no! Holy no! NO! THAT STINKS!'

In Kubla's claustrophobic, helmet-restricted line of

sight, she saw, as through milky glass, her Chief Scientific Officer hammering himself mid-torso, as if attempting to restart his heart, his hopping-about-mad-goblin-spaceman routine lurching across her view, shimmying in and out of clear focus as she blinked tears.

'Holy Shinola,' his voice raspy, but more controlled. 'Mystical pangolin turds! That was baaaa-aaaa-aaad!' She heard his deep gasps in, then whistlingly out.

A tinny beeping coming from her suit let her know something was not at all cosy with the human it was designed for keeping alive. Possibly because Kubla was holding her breath? She let in a tiny sip of air through her nose, gagged hugely, and with a groan of helpless horror swallowed a mouthful of toasty stomach juices with an eyewateringly gruesome gulp.

The planet stink was beyond her comprehension. Like ... No, worse than that.

'Hit your fresh air, pal,' came Zander's voice in her ear. 'It might help. Though if this stink is you've poopled your kenicki's again, maybe not.'

Kubla, grateful for the advice, if not its barb, brought her fist to firmly press the air refresh button mid-chest. Fans in her spacesuit whirred; a hiss brought virgin air from her supply tanks.

'That's it,' from Zander, who was now patting her shoulder. 'Oxy in, stink out. There, there, there.'

After long moments, Kubla stood upright unsteadily, breathing in gingerly. The smell lingered, but faintly, muskily, like a long-pancaked skunk.

'I have never, *ever* had that kind of accident,' she spat, her anger almost unchecked. 'To remind you, this and all we say is being recorded, you dumb ass. You got that? Ne-ver! Now get your hands off me.'

The patting on her shoulder stopped.

Clone Alpha was still in the lander. She spotted his head poking from the door warily.

'Shall I begin SL999.3, Sir and Ma'am?' he asked, with an immense politeness mixed with fear.

'Immediate emergency lander take off, not waiting for return of personnel from planet surface?' quoted Zander. 'Nah, get down here you yellow-bellied swamp slug. Our commander just stood in something, is all.'

'Let's cut the jokes, shall we?' Her mission mind had rebirthed. 'And get a reading on the atmosphere. Clone Alpha, did you smell it up there?'

'Negative,' said Clone Alpha. Then, 'Smell what, Ma'am?'

'Something stinky,' explained Kubla.

'Will you listen to me?' Zander persisted, waving his

arms. 'Why will no one ever listen to me? I always tell the truth, when there's a truth to tell. And I've told you what just happened already! Look under your foot.'

Kubla snorted. 'If you think I'm falling for that …'

'Put it this way,' said Zander, amusement overshadowing the pretend hurt in his voice. 'You smelt it, you dealt it.'

'You are a sad child,' she told him.

'I agree,' he said. 'And also, I am merely informed of a Universal Rule. Which implies that you either soiled your pants, or spectacularly degassed, or, what I'm seeing poking out the side of your right boot spares your blushes, and you merely and quite accidentally stood in something.'

Kubla raised her boot. What looked like a large, half-flattened brown turd hung from it. At the sickening sight, Kubla tasted acid, and swallowed hurriedly.

'Told ya,' said Zander, winningly. 'A planetary whoopsie. *He he he*. How about *that?!*'

chapter
ten

THE WHIFF FACTOR in Kubla's suit was sneaking upwards. She saw Zander punch his fresh air, and so she did the same for herself. Then she scraped the sole of her boot in the dust. The turd shape came off like a twist of hellish clay, and she and Zander hastily punched in more fresh air as they relocated themselves, making short hops in the low g.

'That stuff totally cranks,' Zander commented. Then, 'As does ...'

He'd stopped, and Kubla came alongside him, turning to look back to Big Lander, which was now around twenty hops behind them. Clone Alpha was busy carrying down the first of the sample collection kits, using the straps the way they were supposed to be used, like a backpack. Kubla watched him put one boot on the moon surface, then retract it nervously. He's like a cat on a shiny floor, she thought, wondering if she might remember that line for her notebook, when she got back to her bunk.

'I *said*,' persisted Zander, '*as does …*'

'As does what?' Kubla responded, watching Clone Alpha, still on the bottom rung of the ladder, now not moving at all.

'As does this. And those. And them.'

Kubla turned to him. Zander was pointing at the ground.

'And *thems*,' said Zander, indicating here and there around them, and further off.

'We have to go back for Alpha,' Kubla told him, with their mission in mind. 'He's stuck on the ladder.'

'I'm not!' And Alpha was beside them, his lower half and the whole of one side dusted with pumice.

Kubla started. 'But how …?'

'I hopped too,' the clone explained, with a vigorous salute. 'I'm ready, Ma'am!'

Kubla ignored the clone's weird juju. 'Let's go then,' she said curtly.

She looked into the distance. Everything to the horizon looked moonscapey, with little outcrops of rock you could step over easily – but there was a slow rise to the right that looked … somehow interesting.

'That way,' decided Kubla, waving an arm in the general direction.

'You mean, follow the *footsteps*?' enquired Zander.

Kubla finally looked where he was pointing at the ground. It was a … no. Her mind paused. A shake of the head got some small cogs moving again, but not the larger ones.

Zander was pointing at a footprint. A foot print. Which couldn't be. Her brain shimmied, zoned out for a while.

She found herself thinking of the time someone had told her, for real, that she couldn't be sure, not for an absolute hundred percent, if she wasn't dreaming. Karl Snipe. Blow-dried hair. Held his jeans up with suspenders. This on a trip to Niagara Falls, taking in the Thousand Islands on the way. She'd not liked his angles at all, in the end moved city to avoid him. Of course, when it came to dreaming, she, Kubla Khan, *knew* she wasn't dreaming when she wasn't dreaming, and that's how she knew she wasn't dreaming when she wasn't dreaming! It was simple. If anyone wasn't sure if they were dreaming or not, it was clear as Kansas they should seek medical help.

Or – her brain freeze dragging on a bit – it was like the time in a high school physics lesson when the teacher had suggested light was both particles *and* waves. And maybe other things too. Kubla'd been sent rocking momentarily, but did not succumb. Merely took no more interest in physics, dropped the subject, never considered it as anything more than codswallop.

This was not a footstep she was seeing before her, aha no. It was a footstep no more than Kubla was dreaming and not knowing it, or being illuminated by wafts of frothy waves *and* titsy bitsy particularcules. This was a footstep *shape*. That's what this was.

She peered over it.

It was *boot*print shape, actually.

Her eyes traced the angular marks of the tread. Which formed letters, almost. It was uncanny, she had to admit that.

'MIKEE,' Kubla read aloud, blinking.

There was something else, but she couldn't work it out.

'*Max* symbol,' said Alpha. 'In Chinese simplified character alphabet. Maximum. Meaning: the most.'

'Mikee Max,' whispered Kubla, and her whole world shifted yet again.

This moon ... the previous planetfalls had been so

straightforward. Down here on B3POBOX77 though … or was she only dreaming?

'I *had* a pair of Mikee Max,' she said.

She'd lived for them – lived *in* them! Mikee Max booties, in white. Worn until the loose soles slapped on the pavement like applause when she ran.

'When we left Earth, could you still buy Mikee Max?'

'Chinese mainland,' said Alpha, quoting from his rambank. 'Shenzhen manufacture. Product listing ending year 2088.'

'Brand cheaters!' squealed Kubla, the deliciously sweet memory elbowing itself to the foreground of her mind: she had properly loved her Mikee Max. The market stall rip-offs were even better, more in trend that endless summer of her eleventh year, than the real thing, and when they'd gone to Recycle Heaven she'd cried for days, wanted them back so badly it hurt, almost went to the depot to demand them.

'Nobody in my neighbourhood could afford the real thing,' she told Alpha, and, she supposed, the silent Zander. 'But that somehow made them … even more special for us?'

'Failing to understand,' came Zander's tired sigh,

'that we have, in the now, found *footprints*. That we have been beaten to our plunder.'

'What?' said Kubla, with a frowny scoff. 'You think someone's been here already? From Earth? But that's, well Zander, I think you're barking up the wrong tree there!'

'And why not?' said Zander patiently, pointing to the other prints, showing clearly where at least two people stood, and walked toward the higher ground. 'Why is it not possible someone from Earth was here?'

'Space Lab is the first ship,' said Kubla, flatly. 'So we're always the first.' Then, 'You silly billy!' she added, with a nervous titter. It was not often she beat her Chief Scientific Officer in the brain department ... *so* not often, that she didn't want to celebrate just yet.

There was a pause while Zander drew in a slow, measured breath through his beard. That stinking arrogant pug, Kubla thought, watching him. What's he got for me now?

'Okay,' Zander said, blowing out air in defeat. 'Let's just go with that, shall we? We're the one and only. We're here to collect our samples. Let's just do that. So which way?'

'I would say, make for the rise,' Kubla suggested,

thinking, *Did I win one, or not? I think I did!* 'So we can get a view,' she added, sensibly.

'In other words, follow the footprints?' Zander's tone deliberate and practical.

'Follow the bootie *shapes*,' amended Kubla, sweetly, and, checking that Clone Alpha was right behind her, she enthusiastically led the way.

TRUDGING TO HIGHER GROUND, Kubla spotted, paused, bent and kneeled down every five or so paces, like a toddler on a walk to the bus stop. The result: fourteen small rocks, two ampoules of grainy dust, and a tap on his wrist from Zander to indicate time passing.

Handing the last of her treasures to Clone Alpha, she admitted aloud, 'Poor pickings so far. But we can get a sample of … of … the stinky stuff on our way back.' She mused. 'Some kind of rank mud, do you think? There could be water here … an underground swamp?'

Clone Alpha had set the cumbersome sample collection kit down in something of a hollow, and with its lid closed and bolted, Kubla now sat down on it. As it was purposefully designed for, she thought happily and proudly – it had been another one of her personal choices from the SciTech Accessories catalogue.

Zander was standing farther up the incline, his head haloed by the sunset-orange sky.

'Alpha,' Kubla said, 'why not reccy around for a bit and see if this place has anything else to offer? I need a breather.' And a moment's rest for my poor bladder, she added for herself.

The clone shrugged and walked away, head down and kicking up dust.

Such kicking suddenly grabbing Kubla's full attention – 'Hey!' – Alpha having revealed another of the short turd-shapes, which now rolled sideways down the gentle slope towards her. Kubla's right arm angled towards her suit's air refresh button, but she didn't need to press it: there was no smell.

The turd-shape slow-rolled closer, even kept rolling on the flatter ground until, now only a metre away, Kubla had a sudden realization.

It wasn't rolling, it was *moving* ... the turd-shape wasn't inanimate matter after all, wasn't swamp gunk gone bad ... it was, had to be ...

'IT'S ALIVE!' she screeched, almost wetting herself.

The turd-shape stopped, gave a small wriggle, and,

giving up on sideways rolling, now squirm-surfed the grey-brown pumice like a caterpillar in a bit of a hurry.

Kubla bent from her hips, eager to have a closer look, though not *too* close a one, and declared to it, 'You Are a *Worm*! I Know You Are!'

She sucked in air, and spoke more formally. 'An actual, as in real, as in ALIVE, newly discovered alien life form!'

She took a larger breath in, held it, then: 'I, Kubla Khan, of Space Lab mission, am observing life in the unknown universe. A Space Worm.'

Zander arrived, looked over her shoulder. 'More of a Space *Nose*,' he said. 'Don't you think? Got a hump to it. And two snotters.'

'This is no time for jokes, Zander Drum,' Kubla said, scandalized. 'This moment is … momentous!'

'No, I know,' Zander admitted. 'I'm just saying. It's kind of like a big conk, very obviously nostular in form. Don't you think? Seriously?'

Kubla regarded the animal. Her helmet-cam would be recording, but a verbal on-site record was all important, too.

'Mission log: As advised by Scientific Officer, Zander P. Drum, on closer inspection I can confirm the shape of this life form is reminiscent of a full-bodied human nasal feature, with prominent arch, and two nostril – ish – areas on its forward end ... speculation: eyes? Sensory indentations? *Glands?*

'There, told ya.'

'Thank you for your input, Zander,' she spoke to him kindly.

'Just so long as it doesn't start running,' he said.

She let the silence speak for her.

'It's a nose by any other name,' he said. Then, 'Do you think it has olfactory bits of its own? What I mean is, does the nose *have* a nose?'

Zander nudged the nose-worm with his boot, and instantly both he and Kubla doubled over, thumping at their air refresh buttons. Kubla's stinging eyes zeroed in to see, through her own kaleidoscope of tears, a white fluid wetting the nose-worm's own nostril 'eyes', forming slowly into two almost perfectly-shaped pearlescent drops, which dripped downwards. Kubla shed more tears in sudden over-the-top empathy for the creature.

She said in awesome tones, through coughs as her air cleared, 'Alpha, please return to me. We have a sample to collect here.' Then, with venom, 'Zander, back off or I'll have you arrested.'

Her Chief Scientific Asshole continued, undaunted,

and loudly in her good ear, 'And if a nose hath not a nose, how thus does it smell?'

And answered himself: 'Frighteningly cacky awful!'

A laugh rattled in his throat. Kubla, aiming red-hot eye daggers at him, and not for the first time wishing him to be struck stone dead by a thunderbolt or similar, was gobsmacked to see him suddenly tumble backwards, arms flailing, and hit the ground hard, instantly lost in a cloud of dust.

Was it ... her wished-for thunderbolt? Something similar? Like ... she couldn't imagine.

A thing had ricocheted off Zander's visor and skimmed across the pumice, not far from the returning Alpha. She took a step closer and leaned across tentatively to spy it.

Another nose-worm.

Kubla pummelled for fresh air, her mind adrenalining.

At first thinking that Alpha had really done it now, completely run amok, gone rogue, was attacking his senior ranks with wild abandon and mutiny in mind – and also imagining equally ghastly punishments meted out by Zander for such a reckless disregard of natural-born human authority ... thumb screws ... dangling by feet ... no syrup on breakfast for a week kind of thing –

her train of thought was derailed when Alpha himself was sent sprawling face-first, a deflecting nose-worm arcing skywards, across, as it turned out, Kubla's first view of the moon's pale blue planet rising into an orange sky.

A full-bodied fear surged through her, stilling her moment of astronomical wonder.

The nose-worms were attacking!

Thoughts now turning to her team. Who would lead them? Physicality, wars and violence and suchlike not being her thing *at all*. She didn't even like shaving her legs.

Zander, the useless speck, was rocking side to side on his back in the dust like a tipped-over dung beetle, coughing and whacking his chest controls while broadcasting a long string of sewer words she hoped she'd never hear again.

Clone Alpha, by contrast, had already sprung to his feet – hurrah! He'd removed his bum-bag and belt, and now, in a ninja-like movement, he sent it whipping out, batting away a second airborne nose-worm that otherwise would have connected with his midriff.

Whatever instinct propelled these silent-but-deadly worms, Kubla thought, struggling to maintain an analytical brain over her natural panic, they were both accurate, and purposeful.

Did the nose-worms have *brains*? *Radar*? Did they defend themselves through odour, a kind of noxious chemical warfare? She pulled her head in as one sailed past, and for safety crouched as low as she dared, her bladder protesting greatly.

The nose-worm missiles were coming from higher up the slope, which she currently couldn't see. Imagining an army of them roller-pinning towards her, she risked a stretch of her neck upwards to scan that horizon.

And saw three spacesuit-clad humanoids waving and, to judge from their chaotic body movements, laughing up a hurricane.

'There they are, then,' growled Zander, from beside her, patting his suit down.

'They?' Kubla was aware her mouth hung open.

'*Thems*,' growled Zander, and, picking up the hitherto noncombatant nose-worm that had almost reached Kubla's boot – that first precious evidence of extraterrestrial life Space Lab had discovered – with a caveman's roar he flung it at their enemies, missing the tallest of them only because that one ducked.

And then the smallest of the three assailants gave Space Lab's crew the finger.

Which even Kubla knew meant there was no going back from here.

All six protagonists reached for ammo from the ground, free hands pressed firmly to their chests.

And so history's first known, and still to this date most short-lived, space battle – a.k.a.

The War of the Noses

– began.

chapter
twelve

KUBLA HAD NEVER KNOWN such fun. *Ever.*

She flung madly, heart galloping. At each find of a nose-worm, either by virgin capture or recycled incoming missile, she felt a tsunami-like wave of euphoria seize her, from boots to roots, then stood triumphantly tall, a star jump almost, yells of bloody intent from her throat fogging her faceplate. Twisting then to send the nose-worm in a half overarm towards the foe, eyes squinted and mouth puckered against the pong.

Meanwhile she was a target hard to miss.

Thuck! to her forehead.

'Yaaa!'

Thunk! against her sore ear.

'Yaaa-*oh!*'

She snatched up the mishandled space creatures that had hit her, both now inert as soggy socks, and hoisted them back with attitude.

'Yaaaa-*haaaa!*'

All the while dismissing the guff funk filling her spacesuit, and her gagging.

'*Aim*, dagnabbit!' from Zander, his suit and visor streaked with brown juice, as he pitched a nose-turd, which must have reached its mark. 'YE-ESSS!' he roared.

'Excellent shot, Sir!' from Alpha, athletically catching stink bombs mid-air and returning them, with interest, slingshot style.

Kubla, her hands on her knees while she waited for her air to clear again, and then breathing in huge gulps, lifted her gaze to survey the enemy. She was, if she thought about it, exhausted – spacesuits weren't designed for aerobics, or any kind of throwing, come to that. Sweat ran in beads down her cheeks and pooled saltily at the edges of her smile, where the tip of her tongue found it.

They were winning, though. Had to be, surely. Even if she wasn't aiming, about which Zander maybe had a point. Next time ...

Making a small leap, she caught a stinkpot nose-worm with two hands, landed easily on the moon surface ('Bravo!'), wound up her arm, and sent it back arrow-straight.

This time watched it zip through the sparse atmosphere, and connect – '*Hazzaar!*' she screeched – sending the middle-sized of the three usurpers backwards in an exaggerated, slow motion tumble.

'You *got* her!' Zander cackling insanely. 'Between those freckly blue eyes!'

The other two invaders helped the middle-sized one upright again. *Her*, Zander had said, and perhaps he had a point, the way that one moved.

At which thought the three invaders became more or less synchronized in slowly unclipping hip holsters and drawing out guns.

'Ah, frunk it,' from Zander. 'The gumpjug goosetwangs've gone and spoiled the fun. Just when we were getting our second wind.'

The enemy approached, step by considered step. Kubla wistfully watched recently disrespected nose-worms taking the opportunity to trail away. What, she thought, happened now?

It occurred to her:

'Are they ... *us?*' she asked Zander, pointing at the

invaders. 'From another ... *dimension*?' She was on shaky ground, but had already half convinced herself.

'Sure,' from Zander, dripping sarcasm. 'The Mikee Dimension.'

Kubla bristled, but smoothed herself down. 'Okay then ... *aliens*?'

Her guts melted. The chance of large, animate, thinking multicellular extraterrestrials existing at all was zero point four something – she knew that. But this had not stopped her giant-bug infused nightmares. Not one bit.

'Zander?' she persisted. 'Are They Aliens?'

'Worse,' Zander assured her.

The three assailants stopped six metres from them and raised their guns, each aiming at their counterpart. They were dressed in space lander suits that were rather like Space Lab's ones, only with mirrored silver faceplates, and two fat 'go faster' stripes across the midriff.

'So not aliens?' Kubla checked with Zander. Just to be sure.

'No,' came Zander's short reply through their intercom.

She saw there was a small purple logo writ vertically on the whatevertheywas's left lapels.

'A
m
a
g
o
o,'
Kubla read aloud, curiously. Then, *'Zander!'* she hiss-whispered, conspiratorially like: *'What's Amagoo?'*

chapter
thirteen

THERE HAD BEEN many loves in Zander P. Drum's shortish life. Many.

There was the original and forever saintly Trevor Chumchops.

Followed by Susie the Smoozle Snoozle.

Archibald, he of the blunted tail, cohabited in loving attention with Mister Quibbles, the biter (replaced too soon with Mister Quibbles the Second, a farter).

Most often ghosting through his master's mind, however, would be

His Royal Highness King Henry Scuttlebutt V

the great travelling blue poodle, hit by the bus he was late for, the day Zander left home and never looked back.

Dogs all dying on him.

You loved them, they died.

He'd loved *her* too.

Wished *she* had died.

(Not really, though.)

chapter
fourteen

'AMAGOO?' Kubla was repeating, not sure she was saying it right. 'Ama—goo?'

The smallest and tallest of them – of the Amagoos, Kubla decided, remembering that a thing with a solid name was always less threatening – still had their guns pointed at the Space Lab crew.

The middle-sized of the three, though, who Kubla had decided for sure was female (as had Zander already, she'd noted) holstered her weapon and began fiddling with her spacesuit, somewhere around her bellybutton – if she (or he, or it) *had* a bellybutton. She (or still possibly he, or it) motioned with her head as if to say 'Down here!', and her pals joined in fiddling with their own lower abdomens.

After what seemed too long a time for fiddling at something in silence, Kubla began to stretch her brain for words to open a conversation, in a friendly, nonthreatening but also non-defeatist kind of a way. Before finding her in, though, and with some surprise for sure, a man's voice, baritone, cultured, smooth as milky coffee, spoke in her good ear.

'We on intercom now? Uh? Anyone? Oh, okay I see it now, why do they put that little light there where nobody can ... anyway here goes, am I live? Okay! So here it is: Welcome, Stooges!'

And then a female voice joining in, silkily: 'Have no fear Kubla, Zander and Alpha, we come in peace. We mean no harm. We are friends.'

'Ish!' from a third, junior-high voice, this timed nicely with the smallest of the invaders raising his gun and straightening his arm at the Space Lab crew.

The tallest invader punched the smallest in the shoulder, the baritone returning: 'Put that away, you spliceball.' Then, 'Soz about our clone ... got his codons out of frame, f'yoo akses me.'

The smallest spun his weapon like a six-shooter, blew into the tip of the barrel, and slotted it into his belt.

The baritone adding, genially, ' ... a-and let's be friendly let's say, and even show our faces why not?'

Together, the three Amagoos each flicked their helmet faceplates, their visors clearing centrally to a highly transparent yellow to reveal ... three very human faces.

Kubla gasped. Surprise. Wonder. Shock. Happiness.

From Clone Alpha: 'Hey!'

From the smallest of the three Amagoos, his non-born child's face smiling: 'Ho!'

And from Zander, Kubla noted even while her brain fizzed: nothing at all. Not a zil.

'You're ... *human*!' She automatically pressed her air refresh, for no reason at all, and felt a blush extend from ear to sore ear.

'*And* some,' agreed the baritone. 'You are looking at none other than Commander Brock Veezl, Amagoo StarTime's first launch capitano, six stripes. And as for my crew of baaads ...'

He paused expertly, and Kubla found herself nodding enthusiastically, like a kid watching a funny adult.

'This is Wanda, second in command beside me. And the little fella on the end ... just forget he's here. We left his twin back on ship, and turns out she's the brains of the pea pod they pipple-ippled out of.'

Kubla was aware Commander Veezl, who had to be maybe seven feet tall by the way, still held his gun, though he wasn't aiming it anywhere in particular. Unsure how she should be feeling – relieved, or still frightened – she looked across to Zander.

Her CSO did not look back. He appeared to be staring, fixedly, far off to the left of the Amagoos, out over the moon's bouldered surface of nothing much.

'Are you ... really friends, then?' Kubla dared, taking the initiative. *And what's wrong with you now, Zander?* she spoke in brainwaves, as if she'd recently ticked Number 5 off her Life's Special Wishes list and become telepathic. *Where have you gone?*

'Friends ...' Brock Veezl said thoughtfully, weighing it up, then, 'let's say we are? It sounds more friendly, right?' He waggled his weapon. 'We won the war, we've got the gun ... lame, right? Let's say you're okay and still gonna be breathing coz *we need you?*' A friendly laugh. 'And you need us. We're a team. You'll work with us. For us. *With* us.'

'Erm ...' Kubla uttered, mightily confused.

'You can help collect samples, Brock means,' came Wanda's soft drawl. 'What you're so good at. Delta can lead the way. Would you do that for me, Del? Time, as they say, isn't really on our side?'

The Amagoo clone had already set off, hopping with feet close together like, Kubla thought, Willa the Wallaby herself. She dared not copy, though Alpha was giving it a go, making his way in random hops up the incline, back the way the Amagoos had descended.

Kubla made her feet move. Zander walked with her, small steps. Wanda and Brock parted to let them through, then fell in behind the Space Lab duo.

'You are going to be let's say ay-mazed,' said Brock. 'By our – tell them, Wand.'

'Brock's talking about our tech,' she explained, huskily. 'We don't think Space Lab will have anything like it. Our kit was all developed under great secrecy, and in-house. Private sector. Hush very hush.'

'Oh?' Wanda's voice was weaving strange twinkles in Kubla's brain. Was this – she knew it was – the beginning of something truly wonderful?

'All kinds of let's say weird broohoohoo,' said Brock. 'Impressive, in other words.'

'Of course, it would be fairer to share with everyone,' purred Wanda, 'but that's just the way it goes, I suppose. Private is private. But you're going to love it, Kubla, I know you are. And by the way, I've always wanted to meet you.'

Kubla melted. Who *was* this elfish princess? 'And I to meet you ... I mean, if I'd known about you,' she garbled.

'Wanda's our treasure,' chimed in Brock, affectionately. 'Amagoo's finest star. And by that I mean prettiest. And if that's not an appropriate way to talk, then the world can go hang by its macadamias for all I care. And I do *not* care.'

'Brock ...' from Wanda, as though chiding a favourite parrot.

'No, I mean it. If an ordinary XY guy can't tell a girl she's super XXXX, then before you know it we'll be as extinct as Dilydoes.'

'He means *Dodos*,' corrected Wanda, sweetly.

'I mean what I say, and I say what I mean,' replied Brock Veezl, impetuously, 'it's how the dinosaurs died out, it's how the bees went, I'm telling ya. It's in the DNA. Nobody wants to go extinct-a-byes, right? And that's the whole of biology in a nutshell, free to you, let's say you can thank me later for it.'

They reached the top of the incline at last, and, looking down, Kubla saw what was obviously the Amagoo's camp just a short, steep drop below them.

Two small towers of strap-secured, convert-to-seat collection kits, exactly the same as the ones Space Lab carried but with AMAGOO printed vertically down the sides, stood in an area flattened by footprints. Alpha was down there helping Delta, his clone cousin, unfasten the straps, and lay the kits out neatly in a line.

About a hundred metres distant, Kubla couldn't miss the Amagoo lander, which was identical to Space Lab's Big Lander but with AMAGOO printed vertically down the side.

She wondered what the promised new tech was. The same as she had already, in Space Lab? Surely not. The Amagoo lander was probably chock full of high-end wizardry, she told herself, and could probably zoom all over the place and even back to Earth in a pinch. And what new wonders would they have for sample collection? Her heart fluttered. New things were *mint*.

She felt another flutter, a nervous one, anticipating that she, Earth's biggest butterfingers, wouldn't be able to use it, or else break it, or lose it, whatever it was.

'I hadn't ... heard of *Amagoo* before?' she said, to fill the silence as they descended foot over foot. She was glad when both boots were back on flat ground again. Zander bumped into her, but other than that, he might as well have not been there, for all the use he was.

Wanda touched Kubla's elbow, lightly. 'Oh, we're just like you, girl — intrepid explorers all! We have been following in your amazing wake and are so pleased to have finally caught up with you. This is our first planetfall — we're the newbies here. Can you believe it?!'

Kubla was about to ask more, she had a jug full of questions, but a shout from Alpha burst her bubbles.

'Mikee!' the clone called delightedly, with a wave; he pointed at footprints here and there, and there, and over there. 'Mikee Max! Brand rip-off!'

'Yeah, well,' Brock muttered, sourly. 'Let's say you can't always get want you want. Wanda, quickly now, bring out the really good stuff.'

chapter
fifteen

'IT'S A *LIFE* DETECTOR,' Wanda said, with meaning, and passed it two-handed to Kubla, who dropped it.

Cursing herself, Kubla squatted hurriedly butt-to-heels, muttering heartfelt, panicky apologies to a quite frankly scary silence.

With not even a squeak through her comms, Kubla was left with only the empty *woosh-whoosh* of a bleakest out-of-season ocean – one minus seabirds, children, fun of any kind whatsoever – a white noise set performed by her bad ear, and metered by the baDa—baDa of blood jiving through tubes directly to cheeks and forehead, which she knew were reddening.

The *Life* Detector had split open and lay across a

rock like an oversized shiny black beetle with its wings flipped out, broken-looking, though in some strange way still connected by an oddly angled ball-and-socket hinge.

Kubla, rocking forward onto her only mildly protesting bladder, fully separated the parts by some pulling and twisting, and snapping, then held each piece in her thickly padded palms, staring dully from one to the other, her mind searching for signs of how they might be properly rebuilt into the thing they had cleverly been.

It was the kind of horror from her worst team-building exercise nightmares, and she felt a cold sweat break out in all the usual places.

The piece in Kubla's left hand was about as long and shapely as a superhigh-heeled shoe, but with its heel missing; and where the heel should have been, words were printed – PHOSPHENE LEVEL – in tiny gold lettering. The short piece in her right hand was like a tiny teapot with some kind of button and trigger, but no lid.

She knocked the two parts against each other. 'I can't see ... how they go together?' she admitted to Wanda.

'They won't, sweetie.'

'Oh.' *Crap.*

'Tell me those come in packs of twos,' Brock barked suddenly, standing so close to Kubla she could only see as far as his knees.

'I could lie, dear,' Wanda purred, 'but it won't help you.'

'ASSES!' as Commander Veezl turned away. 'That's ONE STRIKE!'

Kubla watched him marching off, throwing both of his arms about as if to rid himself of pestilence. 'Just go get stuff!' he bellowed, not pausing his stride. 'And if it ain't what I'm happy about, I'll take off and maroon the whole steaming lot of you!'

'He ...' Kubla's mind panicking.

'Would never,' assured Wanda.

'I only WOULD!' came the reply through their linked comms. 'And I WILL!'

Brock reached the Amagoo lander, climbed the ladder, and, as if to purposely turn up the panic dial on Kubla's heart rate, vanished quickly inside at a run.

She looked upwards to Wanda, who held her finger to her visor, and gave a small shake of her helmet. Kubla nodded gratefully: message received. They were safe. It was a just a tantrum, something like that.

Wanda opened her arms in a kind of 'okay, so here

we are' gesture, and addressed everyone in friendly tones. 'Delta sweetie, break out the shovels and picks. And strap-on kits, honeys, we'll be moving ... well, just follow me over this way, I guess.'

Zander shouldered a pack. Kubla, standing again but on painful pins-and-needles feet, copied. Gosh, and her ear was hurting too. The adrenaline of Battle had worn off. Now she was going to suffer. And as for breaking the *Life* Detector ... seven years bad luck? *Seventy*, more like.

Wasn't Wanda a dream, though? Kubla thought. A bestie. A keeper. A wanna *be* her. And for a moment, a NewsReal film showed the two of them disembarking together from a lander rocket, back on Earth, waving madly and hand-in-hand, two mission heroes back home and loving it. Kubla blinked, slowly letting the newly imagined MRM fade from her mind with a delicate sigh.

She was following behind Zander, who followed Alpha, who followed Delta, who followed Wanda. Twisting to look back, Kubla saw Brock sitting in the doorway of the Amagoo lander, his dangling legs kicking idly as he watched them trek out. The fear resurged in her that he might take off and leave them, but she held her tongue. If she asked Wanda again, he'd hear too.

After only minutes they stopped.

'We identified this area from scans,' Wanda purred. 'So just do your stuff. Don't spread too far. Find your patch. Dig. Collect anything you think we might like. Delta sweetie, you get six or seven of them poor odour boys. The rest of you, keep to the smaller stuff.'

'Right – O!' from Kubla. *Poor odour boys*. She grinned. Wanda was such a pleasant person! Rather like herself, Kubla thought, pleasantly.

With collection kits open beside them, the Space Lab team chose miniature picks and spatulas, lined up sandwich tubs, knelt carefully on foam kneelers, remembered their training. Don't pop your suit on anything sharp – keep your heartbeat down to preserve oxygen – and so on, all second nature to them now, on their third mission, Kubla noted.

Our third, she thought. Amagoo's first. *We're* the experts.

She sampled. Scraped up pumice dust, taking a spatula of it and tipping what she could into one of the medium-sized ampoules, then thumbing the lid. Underneath the pumice? Just small rocks, nothing tempting but you never know, so she added a few jagged stones to a bottlette and pressed down the cap, carefully securing both samples in a cushioned rack in her collection kit, working by the book.

Excavating. That was the way. One layer at a time.

She hit harder ground. Jabbed her spatula into it, but could gather no more than a shard or two of the dense substrata. It would do. The others would have more of it, maybe.

She looked about. Her fellow collectors were bent over, doing as she did. It was the scientific way, she thought. Collect your own samples. If yours were duplicates of another collector's, fine. But maybe they weren't. Maybe your sliver of conglomerate contained the exotic microflora or fauna that would revolutionize life on ruined old Planet Earth. Or maybe someone else's sample contained It, the elixir, the Holy Grail, the *rawsch*. The point was, samplers stayed apart. No conferring. Scientific wasn't sociable.

'Anyone got anything superdoop?' Wanda asked.

'Not here, no, sorry not yet,' from all but Zander, who offered only his laboured breathing. Kubla glanced up to see Wanda, who was near the Space Lab Chief Scientific Officer, lean across and touch a palm down on his forearm. Zander responded by brushing her hand away. Hmmm.

A nose-worm nosed a path away from Kubla's fresh scraping, as if, disturbed in its usual routine, it had decided to head for home and call it a day. She thought of nabbing it, but remembered she'd been told to leave those for Delta. And she'd already gotten herself into trouble, didn't want to risk attracting more. The *poor odour boy* was heading for Delta, via Zander, so she was sure it would be collected.

A worm, though!

And she'd been the first. Or, she suddenly realized, the second – or possibly fourth – human to ever see one.

Fourth was ... well, okay, but — her mood deflating — out of the medals and ribbons again, Kubla, she commiserated.

She switched her concentration back to the task at hand. There *had* to be more firsts here. Right beneath the tip of her shovel. Even if it would take later analysis under a neutron microscope to find it.

Bioactive molecules with new chemistries ... she imagined discoveries leading to new cures for cancer, battling plagues, stopping viral pandemics in their tracks. And all from a first discovery by Kubla Khan, space scientist extraordinaire, and her new best pal Wanda ... something ... a fantasy name came to mind:

Wanda *De'lamere*. Her name would be something like that.

'Okay, sweeties, everyone pack up, and let's move my way!'

Kubla re-packed her kit, shouldering it enthusiastically to the next location. Her ear was beginning to spark and, after her next dig, was aflame and throbbing. She gave a small prayer that they might be done soon. At least her bladder was no longer talking to her. She thought: from the exertions of honest and diligent work, and exuberant battle, I have literally evaporated my pee! And giggled.

'No yadda-yadda!' barked Brock, his voice sounding crackly at distance – only the top half of the Amagoo lander was now visible to Kubla. Clearly, however, the Commander was still listening in.

Their fourth location was back down the slope and close to Space Lab's Big Lander, which sat like a friendly bucket of bolts framed by an impossibly beautiful backdrop: a planetary passing, of what looked like a Harvest Moon, glowing red and full to bursting. Kubla, sighing, enjoyed both the sky and their lander's proximity, felt herself relaxing on her home turf. And as she sampled, instinct told her she'd find something different in this location – and there it was, a moist patch of pumice she was nearly sure had to be worm crap. Her heart gave a few strong thumps as, smiling to herself, she slipped a generously filled ampoule into her hip pocket, discretely keeping a hand to her chest to disguise what she was doing, and refresh her air.

'Okay, gang, you're DONE!' from Brock, who was approaching. 'Everybody take five. Clones can pack up.'

Alpha and Delta began hauling fastened-up sample kits back to the Amagoo lander, which was now invisible to Kubla over the rocky incline. She brushed dust off a boulder and sat down. Zander did the same, nearby but a little back from her. Good, she thought. She didn't want to see him. She didn't need his moodiness spoiling this adventure.

'So, shall we do this again?' she asked as Wanda approached.

'Oh, that would be fun, girlfriend!'

'Let's say meet up on the next planet?' Kubla suggested. 'Or the one after ... if you like more ... beauty sleep?' She giggled, again.

Wanda's face didn't respond in kind, only turned winsomely sad. 'Gosh,' she said, 'I've been dreading this bit!' And with a 'this is hurting me a lot more than it's hurting you' look, a flick of her finger mirrored her helmet's faceplate; in which Kubla now only saw a reflection of her own features creasing into a frown.

'Thing is let's say, we just don't need ya,' said Brock, conversationally, his gun loose in his hand.

'We are sorry, truly,' from Wanda. 'We've had such fun. But this is a mission after all. Work. I know you'll appreciate that, Kubla. There's a plan and we have to stick with it. So be strong, lovely. Just – be strong.'

Brock cut in. 'The bottom line let's say is, this little planetary affair has to be *un*-witnessed. As in, by you. We can't have Space Lab turning up Earthside with stories about this, about that, and *evidence* and all that kind of shambooboo, now can we? As in, Hey Ma, Amagoo stole our stuff! We'd be literary – and I mean *literary* – in the tower.'

'We can't ... go home? Where will we go?' Pathetically. Kubla's neck was folded back. She peered up at Wanda and Brock, and Alpha, who Delta was returning to Kubla's side at gunpoint.

'Ye be going NOWHERE,' declared the now piratical Brock, and he raised his weapon to aim at her eyes, double-handed, spreading his legs a mile wide. 'But let's not fall out,' he added. 'How about let's say, I do you a flavour? A bona-fido good *deed*?'

'YES!' from Kubla.

'Sir!' from Alpha. 'Please, Sir!'

'Okay, that's good, so here it is then, and listen.'

Brock paused theatrically.

'You can stay here and suck up the last of the air in your suits, and then die. Or, I can end it for you, here and, as they say, now.'

He reasserted his aim at her face, saying, 'In case of confusion, in other words, let's say, and to put it simply, both scenarios mean you die.'

At which point Kubla closed her eyes, obliterating from sight Brock, the cruel Universe, and everything else besides.

chapter
sixteen

SHE BREATHED IN, she breathed out. She breathed in, stopped breathing for three, and then breathed out again. She breathed in. And then she opened her eyes and hoiked from way back deep in her throat a sog of pale toast, accompanied by a small splash of tea. Watched both slide down her visor a little, and hang there.

Then –

chapter
seventeen

'YOU.'

Brock Veezl, sounding his most commanding. She peered upwards through her bespattered visor.

He wasn't looking at her, had in fact turned his body a little, to point *behind* her.

'YOU, Smart Guy.'

He was talking to Zander.

'YOU are coming with US. I'm told that you could be, let's say, useful.'

Kubla slowly turned her head, like a well-oiled Space Owl, to look at Zander. Her mouth was hanging open, as it had been since she'd thrown her toast. She no longer had the strength or inclination to close it, she thought, dramatically. And why not be dramatical? She could do what she liked now, at the end.

She was to be alone, near as much. Stranded on a moon, maybe at least a twillion miles from home, with a clone for company. They'd watch each other suffocate in their spacesuits. And then it would be over.

She hiccupped.

How had it come to this? She Space Owl'd her head back around and bent over her knees, a hiccupping mess, hair loose and plastered to her sticky cheeks.

Brock started talking again, to Zander, chummily. 'We're totally mostly legit, bud, so no need to worry about getting actually locked up or even zizzed on our return to civilization. Just think Queen Liz, she had her Francis Drake, my main man if you want to know, kind of a hero of mine personally. People say we're alike, but that's a whole other tattle. Just get this: when we return with the spuds and cheroots, we'll be superstars. Just like FD. And they called him a pirate ... ha! HERO, more like. Check your history – no, I bet you did, you know already, you read a book about it. He was ADORED. And they're back home waiting for us ta come back same, you get me?'

Kubla's mind had slowed, everything was s-l-o-w. She blinked. Even her eyelids were slow. Was her oxygen already running low? She hiccupped a last time – it felt like a last time. Her breath was the waft of a lacewing's wing.

'Let's face it,' Brock continued, bending forward from his hips. Twisting on her rock a little, she watched the Amagoo chief give Zander a friendly tap on the arm. 'Life on our ship is the same as on Space Lab, only minus the box ticking and papeywork.' He yawned hugely, and loudly. 'And accountability in all areas, that goes without saying.'

An orthodontist's dream filled Brock's faceplate, which was crystal clear. Kubla, even now in this situation she was in, couldn't help admire her enemy's perfect line-up of pearly whites.

'So tell me who,' said Brock to Zander, 'would not want to be idolized, famous and *RICH*?'

In the silence, nobody moved. She thought: Zander, what the krill is WRONG with you?

'So how about it, fella?' Brock with his free, as in gunless, mitt thrust out, to be shaken, or else to help Zander up from his sitting position, or possibly both.

Kubla found herself tennis-watching, Brock to Zander, Zander to Brock, the rally maybe lasting eight seconds but feeling longer.

Had Zander already died? she thought suddenly.

Had his air long ago ran out? He'd used up so much of it thumping that refresh button, more even than she did. Was that him just sitting there, a corpse?

'In actual fact,' Brock was now confiding exaggeratedly, from the corner of his mouth, as if only to (the dead???!!!) Zander, though the rest of the human and clone population of B3POBOX77 got to hear it fine – and who knows maybe the nose-worms did too: 'Wand rates YOU highly. The highEST. Wants *you* with *us*. Kinky, huh?!'

Kubla yanked her head sharply to the right to regard the female Amagoo employee through one squinting eye. The elf princess. She of the silky milk chocolate voice, who drew you close then stabbed you in the back, and suffocated you and your colleagues. To death.

How Kubla hated her.

She aimed a futile kick in Wanda's direction, and wobbled precariously on her rock. That's for killing Zander, she thought, drunkenly low on breath ... and sent her left arm in a sudden spasm of grief-stricken sympathy toward her late Chief Scientific Officer, her fingers merely tapping the highly toned butt of the Amagoo Commander.

She was glad, now, that she'd let him wear her shoes.

Yes, that.

It was time to admit it. She – Kubla Khan – had let Zander P. Drum, her training partner, put his oafish *unsocked* horrors into her sacred soles, her virgin turf, his pale raw meat squeezed, complainingly, like an ugly sister, into her long sought-after Samuel Choos.

She had not wanted to see a man shoeless in front of his superiors.

That's who she was – or, considering her life was already over, that decision having been made — that's who she had been. A nice person!

Her anger rose to a crescendo, red as the sky behind Big Lander, then crashed, and dispersed, and she was numb, just a thing. With a mensch throbbing ear.

Don't leave me to die here too, she heard herself plead, aloud or in her head, she didn't know, or care. With Zander dead ... *take me instead!*

'How about it, then?' from Brock. 'You coming with us, Smart Guy?'

'Ah, go jig yourself.'

Kubla's mind was in free fall.

Space Lab's undead CSO cleared his throat, but didn't elaborate.

Time had stopped. Have I died too? Kubla wondered, her breath held. Maybe that's it. We're both dead. No, we're ALL dead. The thought comforting her somehow.

Then Brock cursed, something long, violent and unrecordable by Latin alphabet alone – but definitely *pissed-off Tarzan* in tone and lilt. With his left boot he stamped a perfect MIKEE into the pumice before stepping forward with his stamper, closing his outstretched hand into a fist, and giving Zander a deliberate punch to the chest, tumbling the unfortunate but alive Space Lab employee from his boulder.

'See you in hell then, little man,' Brock snarled. And after a swift turn on his heel, he marched across to rejoin his team, his weapon unholstered and aimed at Space Lab's Big Lander.

'I personally couldn't give a finklet,' Brock said airily, 'but had to try, Brownie points from the gal and so on and so forth.'

His finger depressed the trigger of his space gun. No sound, or beam of light, only the door of Big Lander buckling, breaking its hinges, and falling to the ground, raising a storm of dust.

'I only wanted to blow the scumpin' door of,' Brock commenting, as if to himself. He chuckled. 'I'd like to see Brains pilot that funktrug anywhere soon.'

Kubla, watching all, had at some point gotten

groggily to her feet. Alpha hurried to where Zander wasn't even trying to upright himself.

'So it's a goodbye from us,' came Brock Veezl's voice, triumphantly. 'And just as an eff why eye, our Amagoo lander has mucho capability to interface universally, in other words, no hassle with Space Lab's docking bay.'

'You're taking our *ship*?' Kubla now standing with Alpha, who was dragging Zander to his feet by his arm. She looked and saw the Amagoo team's faceplates showing mirrored images of the defunct Big Lander and red sky behind. '*Why?*' She felt like crying.

'Us, inhabit Space Lab? Ha-HA!' Brock now a cackling maniac. 'Sail in that pile of grunking spunknit. No, we're just going to steal the stuff you kindly got for us from the two stops we couldn't be bothered with. XP34 and WEsomething. Saw by hacking your fas-cin-a-ting mission transcripts that you got hold of a bit of this and that, not much, but we'll take it.'

'At least they'll be of some value, Kubla,' Wanda's voice dreamy, soothing, pleading forgiveness, and sounding, to be honest, genuinely upset. 'At least what you've done has had purpose. Won't be wasted.'

The Amagoo team finally headed for the top of the

incline, Brock with his hand held up, showing them two fingers.

But at least not shooting them dead, Kubla thought, guessing he'd simply forgotten.

Disappointed 'Hey' and 'Ho' calls of goodbye from the clones, like far-off departing geese.

Nothing from Zander.

Or Kubla, now. She watched them go, lifting up her inert CSO, holding on to him tightly. Listening to her heart thumping. Or was it his? Feeling utterly alone in her embrace with the never-usually-with-nothing-to-say Zander P. Drum.

Alpha put his arms around them both. 'There, there, there.'

The Amagoo team grew distant, dropped down from the horizon, and were gone.

'Right then,' from Zander, shrugging off his crew mates, 'they're out of direct comms range, so unzip lips and talk freely. Clone Ninja, what's the damage?'

'Estimated damage to Big Lander?' intoned a miserable Alpha. 'It has no door.'

'Gotcha. All other systems?'

The clone peered round the edges of his helmet, blinking. 'All systems report ... hunky dory, Sir.'

'Ace,' Zander said, sounding as cool as a chipmunk. 'Any injuries to self?'

'*We're stranded, Zander!*' Kubla's bottom lip wobbling the words.

His simple joy came through quietly in her good ear.

'He he he heeeee! That's what THEY think. Now stop being clingy, and let's go GET those 'flerds.'

KUBLA STARED after Zander as he moon-trekked over to Space Lab's Big Lander, climbed the ladder, and, whistling tunelessly, went in.

It was as if he'd gone mad. It didn't have a door. Even she could have told him: it would never fly again.

The ground started to shake.

'Oh my jojos!' And she began sprint-hopping, a child left behind, towards the lander, before she was stranded.

She Willa'd over the broken door, two feet together, and tried to make one great, ambitious, desperate leap straight through the blasted-open doorway. Missed by a mile but hit the ladder, and with fast hands finding rungs, scrambled up like a deranged spider, humping her way inside with a kind of dry-land butterfly stroke, followed by a nose-wormy wriggle and sideways roll, coming to a stop by the seats.

'Phumf!'

Within moments she was seated and strapping into her harness.

'Oh, you're in.' Zander spoke from a corner, his body turned away from her.

'You're ... not ... taking off? ' she breathed heavily, and coughed.

'Just taking a pee.' He unhitched a tube from his spacesuit, a small sigh of pressure escaping.

'S'cuse me,' he muttered, mildly. 'Better out than.'

'We have a toilet?' Adrenaline was still pumping. Something in her neck pulsed.

'Strictly speaking? No,' was his reply. 'Kind of improv affair, just don't drink from the regen water tank okay? Why d'you ask, you need a number?'

A shake of her head as, at that moment, Alpha appeared at the top of the ladder, looking pale, and annoyed.

'Oh, Alpha,' Kubla said, realizing what she'd just done, and feeling less than pleased with herself. Before she could apologize for forgetting him, a grumbling roar made all three gather about the doorway in time to see the Amagoo lander blast vertically towards the heavens.

'He he he,' from Zander.

Brains, Brock Veezl had called him. *Smart Guy*. Well, maybe he was. She *knew* he was. Just the sort of head for this kind of emergency. Recovery. Counter-attack?

'So,' she said, nodding towards him. 'We now ... what now we do ...?'

'Glad you're back and needing my help,' Zander quipped with sarcasm, but then seemed to think better of it, and gave her a friendly grimace. 'Sorry you had a bad time with those ...' he waved his arm across the moon surface, and never finished.

Kubla dumbly nodded, the dance of pumice footprints, from above, seeming to her childlike, infantile; their nearly calamitous adventure a thing distant in time already.

Clone Alpha pushed past them both, knocking hard into their suits, and proceeded to kick shut the doors to their sample store cabinets so hard they heard it.

Zander gave Kubla a parental look. Then he said carefully, 'OK, I owes you *both* an explanation, and here it is. Let me tell you the facts, clear and precise –

because time is ticking, as they used to say.' He crossed to a monitor, watched for a couple of seconds, and then turned back to them.

'We are not going to die on this moon. And hopefully not until we've all lived long wastrel lives and grown old enough not to care a diddle anymore.'

'It's going to be fine,' Kubla relayed to Alpha, with a sigh of immense relief.

Zander glanced about, closing another storage cabinet door and running his fingertip down a wall, apparently checking it for dust, saying, 'As you both know, I can at any time call for Really Small Lander to come and get us.'

'We have Really Small Lander!' Kubla erupted joyfully. It was such a tremendously cute little thing; she'd totally forgotten what a bijou sweetie it was. 'And it can come and get us?'

'If I call it down remotely,' Zander said, 'or ask Alphy's sis to do it for me. Remember her?'

Alpha brightened, nodded.

'So whatever happens: we WILL get back to Space Lab.'

Alpha clapped. Kubla, however, saw a fatal flaw in that plan.

'They'll have been there. The Amagoos. They might ... blow it up when they leave?'

A genuine chuckle from Zander, before he changed his mind and conceded, 'No, you're right to be concerned about that, the way they are. They certainly might mess things up a bit, given half a chance.'

Zander abruptly stopped his glancing about and tapping stuff, that he'd been doing.

'They might ...' he muttered, 'go for our personal stuff ...'

She saw a pained, not to say panicky, look pass across his face, and stored that particular tell-tale away for future analysis.

'Which means ...' he said, pursing his lips a second, before, '... it's going to have to be a good old-fashioned Repel Boarders.'

'And we mustn't let them get anywhere near our samples,' Kubla said determinedly. 'I will not have that woman ...'

'Or should we, though?' Zander still with his thinking cap on, by the sounds of it, and by the looks of it too, both his hands now settled on to the top of his head, as if to keep those big old brains from bubbling up too high and escaping. 'If they reach our Locker Room ... they'll be deep inside Space Lab. Deep. And in a confined area. With multiple ins and outs for ... and far to go, should they need to get out ... *fast* ...'

Kubla didn't know what he was talking about, again. 'So what's the plan?'

'Two choices,' Zander said simply. 'First one, bit obvious, but there you go: we unleash Beta.'

Kubla started. It was absolutely certainly the first time Zander had used the female clone's real name.

'Could she ... what could she do?' she wondered.

Zander cupped the chin of his helmet with his palms, and frowned. So did Alpha. They were both looking ridiculously serious. Kubla struggled to know why.

'Too much,' Zander concluded, Alpha nodding hurriedly in agreement. 'She's more ... the nuclear option. No. Last resort only.'

Kubla saw Zander and Alpha lock eyes for a fraction of a second, before both blinked and moved on.

'Really?' she said, starting to smile, but stopping as she felt the pull of hair stuck to the goo on her cheeks. 'Beattie's so kindly though! She might, I dunno, reason with them? *Charm* them?'

'The plan, then,' said Zander, ignoring her, 'will bring into play the Space Lab Irregulars.'

'Eh?' Kubla now completely nonplussed. That

sense of not knowing what she *should* know, like that shoozling feeling of *déjà vu* again, only worse. Were there Space Lab aspects she *didn't* know about? Impossible. She'd been in every meeting. Read every pamphlet. Chosen, by herself and using her particular skill set by the way, its entire range of accessories, from fengshui'ing the furniture, outfitting entire clone wardrobes, everything, all the way down to the duck-in-a-bowler-hat pattern on the mellow-yellow tint 10,000X recyclable toilet paper.

Zander crossed to his flight control console, typing clumsily with his gloved fingers on the large keypad. 'I'm telling Bea to hide in a safe place until it's over.' One more glance about Big Lander's interior. 'And before we arrange troops ...'

Up again, Zander crossed to the open doorway, his right hand finding an unobtrusive panel, about chest-high, labelled with an exclamation mark inside a small red triangle. He pressed his palm on the panel, and when it popped open, stuck his hand inside and turned something. To Kubla's amazement, a new door slid from above, roller blind style, and sealed itself firmly in place.

'Secondary security cover,' Zander said. 'In case of malfunction. Or pillocks.' He gave it a testing thump with the side of his fist. 'Bit of a spare wheel affair, but it will get us to our homestead.'

Kubla watched him. He was like a wizard. A little orangu wizard.

Now he was hunched over his console again, now circling the room tapping stuff, now almost skipping across and sliding into his seat. Finally, 'Right, we're all set,' he said, and removed his helmet and gloves, Kubla and Alpha following his example.

'Smells like sick in here,' Zander commented absent-mindedly, as he reached into an armpit and took out his palmheld. His thumb moved the rollerball back and forth a few times, while a small green light winked on, then started to pulsate.

'Oh, the fun we're going to have, my gang,' he said, to neither Kubla nor Alpha, but turning his attention back to his screen, and typing so fast she couldn't look at his fingers without going all criss-eyed.

'Get comfy, f'I was you,' he said, and after Kubla and Alpha had helped each other strap firmly into their seats, he added, 'Do you want to *see* this, or just *hear* it?'

Kubla didn't understand the question. 'Uh?'

'I reckon just hearing it will be worse. So ...' typing while he talked, 'let's do that.'

He sniffed. 'I'll merge their suit comms units ...'

She heard his hands rattling the keyboard with growing intensity.

'Link the whole lot with microphones dotted around Space Lab ... and by the way did someone puke? No, on second thoughts don't answer ... so we'll hear *everything* ...'

A tremendous roar of keystrokes; and Kubla felt her adrenaline rise sharply.

'So ... and now ... last of all but certainly never *least* ... my dear, my only, my Winston ...'

A finger hit the return key like the shot of a bullet.

'Winston?' Kubla said simply, sounding, she thought, very tired of it all, this still-stranded-on-a-moon lander, this jolly Zander.

'Relax,' her Chief Scientific Officer advised, his fat little fingers now interlacing behind his head, 'and enjoy. The bad boy is coming out to play, and this time ... it's official! Whoa!'

nineteen

CLUNK!

Kubla, sitting overly upright and listening too hard, gave a little jump in her seat. Which was still moon-stuck, while the sounds from Space Lab piped in from somewhere over her head made her home seem maddeningly close by.

pfweeeeew-SHTUMP!

'They're in!' she breathed, heart knocking. 'They've docked!'

Familiar sounds: disrobing, the stowing of helmets on the helmet stow rack, of boots being tugged.

'Just look at this plebs' palace!' Brock Veezl's baritone, dripping disgust, echoed around Big Lander, giving Kubla the shivers — had he just D jumped down here? It was impossible, the stuff of sci-fi, but ... she checked over her shoulders just in case ... no, he hadn't.

'It's the same architectural layout as Amagoo One, almost exactly.' The soothiness of Wanda – Wanda *De'lamere.* Kubla could have spit. *In her face.* 'The docking bay,' Wanda purred, 'the door systems, even the coat hooks all look the same, Brock.'

'The craps they do.' Brock outraged. 'Ours are orange. So, which way? Clone, you go first.'

SHUSTUMP!

'That means they're into Corridor 1 ...' Kubla warned, her voice on the way upwards. Alpha, beside her, nodded sagely.

Kubla's mind traced the path of light footsteps. (And the suppressed thought: are they wearing our *shoes*?!!! Surely not ... no ... No.) Three pairs of feet walking. *Stocking'd* feet, she was almost sure. A louder pair, a middle pair, and a light pair. Padding along.

Kubla thought: The Three Bears are walking into our home. Not *their* home. *My* home! To steal stuff.

The invaders, Brock, Wanda and Delta – in Kubla's mind now with fur on their faces – would encounter three doors leading from Corridor 1. The first led only to Big Research Area and Zander's quarters. They wouldn't take that one, she judged. Oh no.

That door was too large.

And she was right. Onward the paws padded, to the next door, which opened into the personal refreshment room that a person who'd just returned from a long planetfall might find extra-interesting. Kubla, remembering its last user, recoiled at the thought.

'Give it another five-ten minutes, folks!' Zander chuckled throatily from his control seat.

'They won't open that door,' she told him, seriously. 'Too small.'

And she was right again. Onward the soft padding, again, leaving Refreshment Room 2 behind them.

They will never open a door, Kubla was sure, stretching her fantasy to its limit, until they arrive at the one to the Locker Room, which wasn't too large, and not too small either. That door was, for ease of carrying things in and out in the crook of your arm, and sometimes even two arms, *just right* ...

'You *can* stop them getting our stuff?' Kubla bothered Zander. 'Even if they get into the Locker Room?'

'Sshhh ...'

FOOTSTEPS. Footsteps. *Footsteps.*

'Where *is* Beattie?' she queried.

'*Sshhtt!*'

The footsteps had stopped. At, she guessed easily, the Locker Room. Why, what a surprise. Give the gal a prize.

'They are there,' from Alpha, a whisper.

'We are here, Sir and Miss,' from Clone Delta.

Kubla seethed. Go on, hit the green button, you shitinthewoods.

The unlocked Locker Room door opened – *mimf!* – and shortly after, it closed – *mumf!* – with the invaders inside.

The refrigerator-tall secure sample safe would be before them.

A mighty *GONNGGG!* resounded.

'He kicked it!' from Zander, amidst chuckling. 'Hoo-hay what a numsk! Was it for this the clay grew tall? I mean,' twisting in his chair to reveal his huge smile for Kubla, 'some folks just shoot up too far from the ground ... it can't be good for the brain chemistry? To be so high in the atmos? Am I right?' He laughed hugely. She'd never seen him so happy, so ... wide open and free.

It was Kubla's turn to hush him – she'd heard something. 'Zip it!' she said, intent on every sound, her good ear poised to the direction of every brush of cloth on work surface, every sniff or rustle.

Rustle?

What on Space Lab ... *rustled?*

'Brock ...' from winsome Wanda. 'The sample safe is exactly alike to our own. And we don't open ours with our feet much, do we?'

'How'd I know that?' Veezl argued. 'I aint no labcoat.'

'We just need to let Delta fish for the unlocking code.' Wanda sounding tired. 'We'll get the samples, just relax Brock.'

'What kind of froop locks a store chest on a spaceship?'

'*We* do,' came Wanda's reply. 'It's procedure on Amagoo One and Space Lab the same. Delta sweetie, can you open it ... quick as you can?' Her voice faltering slightly, fine cracks in porcelain. 'I ... don't like this place, Brock. It's rather exactly alike, but ... well, not. It has a feeling.'

'It's just this,' Commander Veezl continuing sulkily, 'I'm finding all this Lock Everything vibe ultra-dull boring, can't stand being in here actually, there's a lock on everything and even we're locked in like, I dunno, sardine meat or somethin' that ways.'

'They're sensing it!' Zander with impish anticipation. 'This is going to be ... no, hold back, my lovelies. Let's have a little delayed gratification. We're *owed* it. Digging dirt all day, stinky worm fella slime all up our suits ... '

THUMP!

'Brock! The door has a button. Shall I get it for you?'

'Oh, crumps,' from Zander, hastily lurching over his keypad, rattling off. 'We can't ... have them ... open the door ... to the corridor ... just yet ... he he he.' And, 'No exit, Amigos!'

'Ami*goons*,' corrected Kubla, only afterwards seeing her quip.

'Amigoons!' from a delighted Zander, presenting a palm over his shoulder as if to give her a high five.

Kubla enjoyed her joke. *Amigoons. Amagoons. Amagoonettes.* She was ... randomly spontaneous.

But why wouldn't Zander let them out? They were in her domain. Her workspace. She worked in there a lot. If they want out, let them out!

That sound again. Were their suits brushing against each other? Was Delta doing something ... that rustled? She couldn't make head nor tail of it. Quickly checked the bandage cupping her left ear. Was there some kind of scratchy beetlebug got in there? *From where?*

A loud,

SQUEEEEEEK!

made Kubla's bad ear spasm, before she realized: it was only the storage safe door. She recognized the flimsy thing's clatter as it slammed against the safe's side, a bump as it swung back again in its poorly lubed hinges, which never did seem content, and now after having a Brock Veezl kick aimed their way ... she almost knew how those poor hinges felt. Intimidated. Violated. Thrown out of kink.

A long, gritty scrape as a tower of giant-sized airtight sandwich tubs, heavy with their contents of dust and stones, was tugged out.

'That's our samples ...' she warned.

Zander only raising his hand for silence.

She listened. The rustling had ceased. The Amagoons were – holding their breath?

'It's time,' said Zander, lifting his palmheld for her to see. 'Ready to move on my count. A-Four. A-Three. A-TWO elephants. And last, and also least ... the lucky number ... a-One!'

He thumbled the rollerball.

'Activating Space Lab Irregulars!' he roared, turning

his devil's face, featuring his newly discovered world of pleasure, around again for Kubla to see.

She did not like what she saw.

His eyes, shining wetly in the corners. His hurried blinking. His regretful, though still joyous, wink before, 'And sorry, Alphy baby, it's ears off for you, you delicate little soul, you.'

'Affirmative,' from a grateful Clone Alpha, who covered his head with his arms, and then crossed his legs too.

After that came what Kubla would later refer to only as The Noises.

Rustling, rising to a pattering, and pattering to a scattering, and the scattering giving way to – a yelling, and a screaming. Most notably the intense soprano ululations of Wanda *De'lamere*, Amagoo's second-in-command, and all round wicked witch but poor, poor thing; and the THUMP-THUMP-THUMP of Brock Veezl – who else? – trying to open their exit the only way he knew how.

'Rats – RATS – RAAAAAAAAAATS!' Wanda opera'd.

Amidst such clattering mayhem, Kubla's own voice rising sky high above all, her words resounding with such a thunderous power that her command was executed without a moment's hesitation: 'ZANDER P. DRUM YOU LET THEM OUT RIGHT THIS MINUTE!'

Her mind then left ablaze with the flicker of imagined scenes, a memory reel she would spend years erasing. Ear pained with the shrill and nightmarish retreat of the Amagoo crew from Space Lab, while Zander bounced in his pilot's chair, singing gleefully an impromptu soundtrack he had of course mostly stolen:

'RATS!

They fought the dogs, and killed the cats – ha!

And bit the babies in their cradles – ha!

They ate the cheeses out of vats,

And licked the soup from the cooks' old ladles!

Knocked over kegs of salted sprats,

Made nests inside men's Sunday hats!

And even spoiled the women's chats,

By drowning their speaking

With shrieking and sq-sq-squeaking

In fifty different sharps and f-f-f-flats – AHA!'

Kubla aiming vicious kicks at his chair all the while, in her fury at him, only drawing herself back as she thought of the old saying: that revenge was a dish best served cool, was what the saying was.

'Robert Browning's *The Pied Piper of Hamlin*,'

Zander admitted. '1842. A bit dated in, let's say, attitudes, and so on, and — let's say — so forth.' His mimicking of Brock-speech uncanny.

'Uh-huh really?' Kubla responding lightly, with a calm look toward the back of his head, and a narrowing of her eyes nobody saw.

chapter
twenty

SPACE LAB'S CAMERA 5 SHOWED, in grey tones, an empty, curving Corridor 1 that was decorated with dark marks, as though graffiti punks had flicked paint from their jerries as they'd torn past.

It was *almost* artistic, Kubla thought, for a moment not thinking what the marks actually were.

A dead, squashed and visibly boot-printed rat – those who hadn't known it personally might have inferred that its given name had been MIKEE – was being dragged away by a brother, one or other of them trailing something that identified itself to the viewer as intestines, or similar. The rescuing rat was rather unusually large, and wore headgear consisting of what looked like a scrunched tin foil hat encrusted here and there with two-millimetre nanochip control boards, held on to its head by a wire chin strap.

Zander hastily switched cameras, but Kubla, watching from her seat in the still moon-bound Big Lander, had seen it. Oh, yes. That unusually large rodent with helmet and control boards, she had *seen*.

Space Lab's Chief Scientific Asshole had already fast-forwarded quickly through the camera footage, not dwelling – thank Tana, thought Kubla – on the gory bits.

Or was he just keeping those horrid images for later, for himself? For a private viewing? Maybe. Yes, maybe he was.

Whatever his foul reasons, Zander had only slowed the video to real-time once he'd reached the period *after* the Amagoons (as she now only thought of them; the descriptor had stuck like gum) had de-docked their lander and zvooshed back into whatever bit of space they'd crawled in from.

Kubla was finding it hard, however, to forget these final fast-forwarded seconds, which seemed to want to repeat themselves across her retinas – the mini-movie showing the three until now rather-cool-about-their-movements invaders doing, in full lander suits, and somewhat restricted in the 3-metre-square docking bay, a selection of frenetically madcap dances that might have been named *Quickly! Get The Helmets On!* followed by, *Oh no! There's Rats in Our Boots!* and as a finale, *Hey! Don't Bite the Clone on the Bum, Chum!* as they were harassed, nipped and generously terrorized by at least two dozen leaping fur-enemies.

'Aerobic,' Zander had commented, dryly, at the time, waiting for the speeded-up humans to hurriedly exit screen right, and the rats to ... well, they were there one half-second, gone the next; Kubla had nada ideas about that yet.

Zander had then scrutinized the empty docking bay footage at length, for several minutes even, only reeling along to the bespattered Corridor 1 when he'd noised a guttural grunt of satisfaction.

Kubla heard him repeat the grunt. Corridor 1 was, she translated, to his satisfaction also.

Then suddenly, Zander barked, 'You in there, clone?'

The door to Refreshment Room 2 opened and Beattie appeared, with a grin and a thumb's up. She was holding, weapon-like, a many-bristled toilet brush, and wore on her nose a small flower-shaped clothes peg with a sunflower motif, one of Kubla's — and from her personal laboratory drawer, no less, its sole function until this latest innovation being to hang up wetted nopaper towels on a washing line of string, for reuse.

'Nice one,' from Zander, and Beattie gave a small curtsy as she removed the peg, slipped it into her trouser pocket, and tossed the toilet brush over her shoulder.

The next camera view showed inside their Big Research Area laboratory. Zander carefully rewound and replayed footage, taking more whole minutes before moving on.

'It's fine. They didn't go in there,' said Kubla, impatiently. 'We need to see where they *did* go.'

'Better safe than,' replied Zander, dourly.

Finally, Zander found her the Locker Room, and Kubla leaned forward in her seat, mouthing an almost silent, 'At last!'

What she saw made her want to cry. Her stool and bench equipment were strewn about as if a tornado had kicked off in there. The sample safe door hung crookedly, seeming to have passed into its next life. The storage tubs themselves were, thankfully, still in a heavy stack, but they'd definitely been touched, handled, tugged at, bruised about the edges. And on top of the stack, like a discarded limb almost ...

'Is that ... a clump of *hair*?'

Zander rigid, then slumped. 'Ah, Goldilocks took

her helmet off, o'course she did.' He sighed, with tones of regret, Kubla thought. A slow shake of his head. 'Well, she's only missing one lock of.'

Kubla was wide-eyed, transfixed by the shock of white amidst the grey. She felt repulsed, triumphant, appalled, self-satisfied, amazed. It confirmed what she'd already imagined. Wanda De'lamere was blue-eyed and blonde, would have to be. And she'd have the *most* fun. Had to. 'She's blonde,' she said, aloud.

'Say what you see, why don't you?' Zander's sarcasm had returned, with a renewed sharpness.

'Long hair ... tied back I assume ...' Kubla thoughtful. 'We have to keep ours short. On Space Lab.'

'And you do as you are told so impressively,' from him.

'What? Oh ... and you ... you know what, Zander,' the height of her tolerance breached, 'you, are a trunchfunklumping Floont!'

'That's my girl. Now, how about I get us home?'

And without warning, he launched Big Lander skywards.

<h1>chapter
twenty-one</h1>

BEATTIE WAVED at them excitedly through the docking bay doors while they confirmed gases and pressures, and suited down to their Skinz. All the while Kubla welcoming exhaustion at last, tingling all over with it, feeling her face muscles relax, her eyes droop.

The smiling clone held a yellow cleaning bucket up to her chin, and was repeatedly raising her thumb, while Alpha grinned back enthusiastically, a child just back from a school trip.

Thank Tana for clones, thought Kubla. She'd seen nothing of the gore she'd imagined waiting for her, because the resourceful Beattie had erased all evidence of the Amagoons' retreat, every last minchin. Floors, walls and surfaces gleamed like a TV advert, and there was the faintest smell of cleaning spirits, reminding Kubla of her Grandfather Khan, and his collection of empty brandy bottles kept at the bottom of his wardrobe.

Nobody had spoken on their return journey. Zander had been intent on his dials and screens, seeming to Kubla rather over-interested with views of Space Lab's external docking area as they approached, inch by inch.

I'll get you a picture of that for your ceiling, Kubla almost quipped, surprised by her sarcasm, but not really, she was as tired as a funkdog.

She sat her butt down on one of the spacesuit crates. They always reminded her of those old travelling trunks, from Dickens knew when, and momentarily her tired mind paused to imagine a steam train tooting off from a station, before she dragged herself back to the here and now and heaved and pushed the last of her spacesuit over her boots, the boots coming off too, and that was about it, she was done.

Her throat was gruesome, and she needed a drink, a cold one. She pulled on her leggings and slipped her feet into her gumboots. Draped her white string cardigan over her shoulders.

'Can I – go first?' Zander apologetic. 'I just want to ... check a few things?'

She nodded, waited for him to finish putting his jeans on and jar his monstrosities into long-defeated pool sandals. He'd have his reasons to 'check a few things', and she didn't care a hoot what they were. She might even go straight to her bunk and get under the covers. She felt her body sag in anticipation, a soft groan escaping through her parted lips.

Zander pushed through the docking bay doors, gave a small nod to Beattie, who was waiting to hold hands with Alpha. As Kubla followed, squeezing past the twins, she gave a little snort as if to say, 'Well, that was hairy – but all's well that ends well!', thinking only of cool liquid in her mouth.

He – Zander – crept up and down the now pristinely clone-cleaned Corridor 1 like a beggar looking for a penny, did the same about the doorways and the edges of doors. Inside their Big Research Area laboratory he crawled under benches and around cabinets. Kubla had never seen him so busy.

'You think someone's still here?'

'Nah I don't,' he replied. 'Just can't stand the thought they'd left anything behind.'

She followed closely after him into the Locker Room.

'Other than,' he continued, 'what we already know about.' Pointing to the lock of hair, which lay forlorn and untouched on the tower of sample store sandwich tubs.

Beattie and her bucket had clearly done the rounds in this room too, but the fateful calling card of Wanda De'lamere lay untouched. Whether the clone had been instructed to do so by Zander, or merely used her intuition, Kubla could only ponder.

'About which ...' Zander taking the initiative and, grabbing a green paper towel from a dispenser, used it to snatch up the blonde tonsure and deposit it into the waste flap in the wall, before pocketing the paper towel.

'And that's the end of that,' he said, and, 'Now I'm going to soup in my sack for fifteen hours.' Turning to Beattie, who stood with her soulmate in the doorway. 'Wake me up during that time, and for what isn't a life/death emergency?' He slowly drew a finger across his neck, letting his tongue loll out.

'I'm poopled too,' said Kubla, to Alpha. 'So same for me. Minus the threats,' she added pointedly, but Zander had already brushed past everybody and was walking away to his quarters.

'And thanks for saving us, by the way!' she almost sent out after him, but a flash image of the rat in the scrunched hat dissuaded her.

'M-Miss?' from the clones, heads cocked.

'Nothing,' said Kubla. 'Now, you two get ready for bed too, won't you? No staying up, okay? Tuck yourselves in. Dream ... ' she was too tired for this ... 'nice things.'

And minutes later, wrapped in her bed linens, she dreamed immediately of being back on B3POBOX77 with Brock Veezl standing over her, toting his gun at her, wanted her to get up, which she wasn't going to, not ever. In her dream, she took an egg from down by her feet and threw it at him, all over him, and that set Wanda to telling her off, and asking how they could ever be friends if she was so unreasonable all the time?

And then the rest of them shot off in the Amagoon's lander, now orange as a bottle of fizzpop, with Zander waving goodbye to her from a porthole. They'd wanted him, not her ... and she couldn't breathe.

She turned over in her single bunk, a clearing nostril opening up a much-needed air supply. And saw that Zander was there, standing over by the wall of her room, in his full lander suit.

'Ah, I never liked those gumpdangles,' he said. 'It's better here.'

And then he had yellow hair. And overgrown, six-toed bare feet.

Which is dreams for you.

chapter
twenty-two

THERE WAS AT THE TIME, and still is to this minute, the question of, 'Why?'.

As in, 'Why was Earth's first deep space starship sent off with the born persons Kubla Khan and Zander P. Drum inside of it?'

Some said the ConChooSpExers, a.k.a. The Old Dudes, were insane. By the end of the Great Choosing, I mean. Of Kubla and Zander. But you don't know anything about that, do you?

Sigh.

Okay, as if we all didn't have better things to do ... here goes.

The decision about *whom* to send on a mission into space that would boldly go etc. etc. etc. and probably not come back, was based on more than 80 years of peer-reviewed scientific research, comprising more than 1.2 billion mostly butt-achingly boring words.

Which had to be mined and sifted. To find the gold in it, innit.

For the industrial-strength document digging, seven *Notables* were drawn from the seven major branches of advanced human research, which at the time – we're talking late 21st Century, ish – were Biology, Chemistry, Physics, Ecology, Mathematics, Astronomy and, just in case, Astrology.

Now, as everyone doesn't know, prospecting research of this magnitude takes periods of time not uncommonly measured in *life*-times.

The elected *Notables*, at this point late middle-aged and with declining juice left in them, agreed to selflessly dedicate their remaining days, and quite likely their last due decades, to the cause at hand.

Such agreement signed in Blood-Ink, so you know.

Tasked daily with mammoth meta-analyses, deep-thinkingly dinosaurious foresights, and common and garden weasel bickering, they proceeded towards an eagerly awaited conclusion that would give the 9.7 trillion dollar Space Lab Mission the maximum chance of success.

The *Notables,* soon renamed the Consortium for the Choosing of Space Explorers (the ConChooSpExers), a.k.a. The Old Dudes, were housed, due to it's a long story, in a purposely converted Holiday Inn in Barnsley, in the United Kingdom, for the duration of their endeavours. They were promised all they would need in terms of resource, and advised not to go out and mix much.

Their *First Conclusion* came to light after only eight years and nine months of frowny work, and took into account research studies from the 1980s that included sensory deprivation experiments, closed community living, sensorily deprived closed community living, and what mice do. Here it is in full:

How Many to Send on Space Lab Mission: Answer: 12 agouti brown, fifteen albino & 6 long-tailed

After a one-year Rapid Consultatory Period, and plenty of media chuckling at their expense, The Old Dudes came up with their *Addendum to First Conclusion.* Here is that in full:

Okay 2 born persons then

Which had been widely anticipated after someone had told everyone that the construction of Space Lab had been underway for over a decade, and any more than 2 persons wouldn't fit, unless the extra wanted to live, (a) in the crawl-in attic space above the fusion cells, or (b) on the outside.

So 2 born persons it was.

To stop the 2 born persons going nuts by Wake Up 6, a TV evangelist had the idea to bless each of them – whoever they might be – with a clone, to do the work, and to pet as needed. 'Like cats,' his vid-report finished, and to illustrate his point cutely, he drew for the viewers two felines, but forgot to put the ears and tail on both of them.

And so The Old Dudes ordered a pair of clones to be delivered on-time, plus one attic-sized bunkbed.

And meanwhile they turned their attention to the characteristics 2 born persons should embody for maximum mission success.

After only seven more years, the results were in.

To honour each Old Dude's contribution, and strictly according to contract, characteristics were listed alongside the speciality of the particular Old Dude who came up with it. Here is their report uncorrected and unabridged:

Characteristics for Space Explorer's:

+2 (Mathematics) <3% plastic (Ecology) neutrino-transparent (Astronomy) Piscean (Chemistry), pH6-8 (Astrology) non-magneticoidal (Physics) warm-blooded but mostly hairless (Biology) born persons.

The search for such entities now began in earnest.

The Old Dudes' Big List On Paper numbered tens of thousands of PhDs and shining stars of academia; these were whittled down, over half a decade, and by many criteria (affability, team players, okay with spiders) to just seven perfect candidates. With only 2 persons needed, The Old Dudes celebrated, the evening before face-to-face interviews, with a night out in Barnsley Town Centre, finishing late into the evening with cocktails at Peppermints, and an hour hiding out in the police station.

Reason for subsequent failure: all seven candidates interviewed said no.

The Big List On Paper (B) came more quickly, and was comprised, with clear desperation, only of those with the lowest personal integrity. Fame Mongers,

Narcissists, Jackals, Money Grabbers, Post Office Counter Workers, and Floonts.

Reason for Strategy B Failure: the insular Consortium didn't know any.

A blank piece of A4 paper, the results of half a year's work, was hastily shredded.

The Big List On Paper (3) was collated of types of person of no use to Earth, or anybody on it, who would simply be forced to go, either by planetary peer pressure, or threats. The candidates sought included *but were not limited to*: political leaders of any country; long-distance swimmers; and anyone who had more than fifty bowls and plates pushed under their bed.

Reason for Strategy C Failure: Health & Safety concerns they might breed up there, evolve into something nasty, and come back.

And so the seven Old Dudes grew old, real old, and one or two of them wondered if it wasn't a fantastical mirror they were condemned to stare into, and that, in fact, the seven of them would, finally, be forced to choose themselves, and go into space, and live in cages, crawling on ancient boneysore knees, turning hamster wheels by day, sleeping by night balled up in little plastic houses ... in short, they were getting emotional and feeling sorry for themselves, for the chunk of their lives that lay wasted.

At this time they were known to wander the streets of Barnsley, looking pretty much like everyone else there.

In last ditch desperation, The Old Dudes petitioned for a move, and found themselves in Space Avenue Complex, Menlo Park, California, in the USA. Which is where everyone wants to be in the first place.

They negotiated use of the conference room on mornings Monday, Wednesday, and Friday, with cookies and coffee included.

Time to Space Lab launch was: nine months.

The search for personnel was shockingly overdue. And yet strangely it was *not yet* a scandal.

It emerged later on that Earth's minds, both busy and not, had assumed that the Space Lab crew was chosen yonks ago, of astronauty, sciencey types, and that those space heads were being whizzed about upside down and back to front, and doing whatever else they needed to do, by way of preparation.

This fallacy in hive-thought was only brought into question when one Ozetta-May Grute, aged seven and a half, wrote to ask the supposed crew some questions (What's your favourite colour? Have you ever held your breath? I have, for nine seconds, etc. etc. etc.). Thus in reply to an innocent child – and the subsequent sale of the Grute family's discovery to media worldwide – the sad secret was revealed.

Space Lab didn't have a crew yet.

Such a sensational fact reached as far as 6th place on the RealNews News Chart for a whole morning, before falling south when somebody's lips exploded.

However, the 'Space Lab Crew Boob' news was out, and by strange serendipity some Australians (people of a nation located a long way from anywhere else and they prefer it that way) found themselves putting *their* oar in.

Or at least, the Budgie Chronicle did. The self-styled 'last real newspaper on Earth', the Budgie Chronicle, serving the mining communities of Budgie and Little Budgie, New South Wales, Australia – 5 hard copies printed weekly, and one of those was to tear up for the Little Budgie K-ute Koala Rescue Lounge refreshment corner – quoted the Australian Prime Minister's exasperated words on the matter: 'Why don't they just put a couple of H.E.R.O.E.S's up there, for heaven's sake? Or am I a Neocretian Sponge or something?'

Mention in print, even incorrectly, of The Neocrete Sponge guaranteed viral status, and for a few hours after digital upload, several million of those persons with nothing else to do debated the Australian Prime Minister's point, globally.

Of course it should be a couple of H.E.R.O.E.S. (the opinion of this audience was heard to shriek) – it just *can't* have taken thirty years for some Old Dudes to work that out! Why, if they'd asked me this morning before breakfast, I'd have told them: 'Put a couple of H.E.R.O.E.S. up there, for moop's sake!'

Now, then.

And now then some more. And when we're ready, now then again.

Think of around two dozen ex-military pilots turned astronauts-with-full-training. Now imagine they're part of their very own Exclusive Club.

And imagine they tell everyone their Exclusive Club is known by their self-thought up acronym, H.E.R.O.E.S.

And imagine they get on daytime TV sometimes.

And now imagine that's the truth. No, really. T.H.E. T.R.U-ooth.

And now you're there.

The H.E.R.O.E.S. had, in their supreme confidence in themselves, believed they'd be shoe-ins for the mission, as they were the only *actually qualified* candidates for the rigours of space flight. Indeed, the relatively fresh-faced and eager Old Dudes had initially thought so too, and had long ago invited a contingent to Barnsley for a serious chat.

Subsequently needing several months to get over it.

Following the Australian Prime Minister's confident outburst, The Old Dudes now approached the H.E.R.O.E.S. a second time, with tones of reconciliation, and booked an airy, pleasantly *Menlo Park* room to welcome them in.

With the same outcome.

This time releasing an emotional statement.

'We've met with them *twice* now. Come on, guys, you've heard and seen them too. Give us a break!'

And everybody suddenly seemed to understand.

The media, however, took this planetary sized failure as a call to arms. Shows were commissioned, celebrities rounded up to present them.

On *Starships in their Eyes* (Channel 45) a pair of notorious but affable *pseudoscientists* were considered for the trip, though mainly because there wasn't anything else to be done with them, apart from some fun bombarding them with short frequency radio waves and observing what didn't happen.

Television presenters themselves were mooted. Chimpanzees in captivity were spoken to. For another precious month, the mice idea was gone over again, in the form of a nightly cartoon nobody could ever remember the title of, which imagined for its audience exciting mouse excursions to planets made, rather too frequently, of cheese, and one time, in bad taste, of ham.

Finally, on a Tuesday in Menlo Park, four weeks to launch, The Old Dudes reached the end of their long tethers.

'Flange and jellyfunk it,' they said, and similar; they were now just a circle of hags crouched in high-back chairs, worshipping at a crumb-scattered conference table, with not a biscuit for their scheduled meeting to be had, or a fresh coffee urn: *who do we know?*

At which moment Kubla from Purchasing entered the room, carrying twin armfuls of folders to be perused, schedules and stationery order forms to be box-ticked, and as she wriggled in, old, old eyes met across dark oak. Chins moved slowly down, then up again. Aged, caffeine-deprived minds were given hope of life by the pursing of lips. And finally – and *finally* –

the corners of mouths unanimously, and gratefully, spread.

'Let me ask you,' rasped that day's Chairperson, of Kubla, who had just put down her paperwork, and was pressing creases from her soon to be considered lucky pale pink leggings, the ones with the red lipstick kisses running up and down them.

'Yes, Ma'am?'

'Ever wanted to go on an *adventure*?'

Who to send *with* Kubla Khan was as easy as pee, and took only minutes to decide, thanks to the insight of Joss Klaff, or Josey to her friends on the Consortium for the Choosing of Space Explorers, which by now included the whole lot of them.

'How about ... there was this guy I met with once. Just a kid back when ... but, and you'd never know it to look at him, his IQ score was 449. I joke ye not. Beyond even any feasible maximum, no matter which way you look at it.'

'So?' wondered aloud the astronomer sitting across from her, foggily.

'*So*,' replied Josey, 'how about *him*? With *her*?'

'The brains and the ...' politeness prevented the

thinking-aloud Consortium member, a chemist who'd had half a finger bitten off by he'd never say what, from finishing.

Stomachs were gurgling. Kubla had yet to return with their promised biscuits. Or fresh coffee.

'Do we need to *see* him?'

'Couldn't care a fart.'

'I vote we vote.'

'I second that. And hurry along, or I'm going to just crunk and die here. I want to spend time with my family before I'm sucking my Thanksgiving turkey up a straw.'

'Okay, hands up who – '

The speech was stopped by a sudden show of hands, the fastest any of The Old Dudes had moved in a decade.

'Well then, Josey, your wunderkind just got another highly unlikely score!'

There was a round of soft, self-congratulatory applause.

'He got a name?'

'Drum,' said Josey, with a broad smile. 'Zander Something Drum. Cute, ain't it?'

'A-and ... has this genius got an ounce of *emotional* intelligence, *social* intelligence?'

'Not a jot,' said Josey, and she gave a giggle, the

sound a pleasant trickle emerging from her desert-dry mouth, and one that was echoed by all six of her ancient colleagues on the Consortium.

All well and good ... so far.

Yet following that ripple of joy, and in a strange synchronicity alike to some branch of physics nobody's thought much of yet, The Old Dudes began to shake, such shaking visible as seven sets of crone shoulders pistoning up and down, hesitantly at first, as if they hurt doing it, but with a definite and defined, though for now silent, *rhythm*.

And then, as if that was never going to be enough, those shoulders loosed tight ribcages, whose bony stirrings nudged into activity long under-exercised diaphragms. And with an awakening of these instruments of sound, the Consortium's initially harmless humour found an unnerving volume which grew swiftly and kept growing.

Those unlucky enough to pass by the conference room doors at these moments described the sound they heard as quite similar to (a) Dry-throated Banshees from the Old Country, a-howling for the dead, (b) Muttley, or (c) None of the Above but I was scared by it.

Within the conference room itself and about its circular dark-oak table, events now moved apace.

Until recently in a state of near hibernation, lungs as tight and crackly as scrunched potato chip packets were suddenly over-inflated in lurching, gagging spasms, only to immediately expel their rude intrusions in gaping, guppying guffaws. Further draughts of stagnant conference room air were sucked in, each to burst out rheumatically, now as barks, now as yelps, now as yips, now as impossibly tragic yodels, while elixirs of rejuvenated blood soared into bat-crappy craniums, to be sloshed up eagerly, and drunkenly, by oxygen-thirsty brains.

And then The Old Dudes roared. And could not stop.

Three of the seven died that day, happily. And that left four to dodge bullets in short retirements, all of whom were granted the time to enjoy with their own eyes the launch of the pristinely shiny Space Lab, carrying its born persons two, namely Kubla and Zander, from Earth and into the darkening sky. These four even lived to sneer goodbye, exactly twelve months later, to the private-enterprise funded and decidedly dodgy Amagoo One.

News of neither of the ships, or their crews, was to be heard of again by even the longest-lastingest of the near fossil Old Dudes still standing. And did that old deary give a whizz? They certainly did not.

An internal inquiry into the *Space Avenue Complex Conference Room 'Old Dudes' Affair*, by some people, and published in the 960-page Space Polity Official Document on the matter, determined that, on reflection, the lack of biscuits probably had nothing to do with it. Though others claimed privately that the poor provision of snacks was significant, and had at least started it, so there.

chapter
twenty-three

'I'M NOT good when things don't go right,' Zander said as soon as Kubla entered the room that was at this point in time referred to as The Watsit Room; previously The Room With No Name; and before that, This Place Whatever Its Name Is Supposed to Be. Uniquely *unnamed* in Space Lab's blueprint, it was notable also in its exclusive use by the crew's two born persons. Clones – and, Kubla presumed, rodents – were not permitted. At least, she'd never seen sign of either.

Zander was standing at the wall vendor. He was wearing knee-length silken boxer shorts of a viral snot-green colour that were mostly covered, thank Modesty, by a washed-out black XXXL-sized band T-shirt. Crossed electric guitars outlined in spider thread were still shyly visible; when he turned away, she was treated to the view of a human skull with a snake snaking its snakey way thought its eye sockets. Kubla did not let her gaze drop to Zander's feet, knowing from past experience they would be uncovered.

Partly to distract herself from ugly-toed imaginations, she concentrated her attention on the upper garment: that T-shirt looks a hundred years old, she thought, and quite possibly not his. Maybe he stole it from a goth giant! Such an idea giving rise to – but she clamped her mouth shut with her hand, found her notepad where it was supposed to be, fumbled it open one-handedly, and made sure she got her witticism down exactly right:

Maybe he swapped it for his shoes!!!

Hurrumphing behind her fingers, she stowed the notepad away. She felt light and nineteen again. Skittish. A long sleep had done her the world of good.

Zander's paper cup was filling its last with the intermittent noise of an ancient donkey peeing into a saucepan. 'Want one?' he asked.

'I'll get mine,' said Kubla, keeping her tone neutral. This was no time to pick a fight. A fight before bedtime was never resolved. Her mother had told her that.

'Sure,' he replied, easily.

Kubla let him take his drink over to one of two paisley pattern armchairs, then keyed in a code for her own nighty-night beverage, and waited patiently for it to be mixed and squirted. Unique to her metabolism, the nighty-night was a necessity, not an option. If you didn't drink it, you didn't make it out of suspended animation. It wasn't just a pick-me-up, it was a get-me-up, she thought idly, lifting her cup and taking a sip that burned the tip of her tongue.

The drink also had some sleep draughtiness to it, not really part of the hibernation, but just to get you thinking it'd be a good idea to get your head down like a good little lamb. A feeling she much looked forward to.

While she waited for the hibernation vibes to kick in, she joined Zander across the tartan plastic coffee table that attached to the floor, sitting in the armchair she'd always sat in, which she supposed therefore made it hers.

'Only bit o' this thing we do I actually rate,' Zander said, sounding already woozy. He held up his paper cup and saluted her with it, then downed the last of it, burping healthily. 'Even quite like the taste.'

'Strawberries,' Kubla said, sipping from her own cup daintily – you weren't supposed to lug it. She touched the sticky plaster on her ear; the suspended animation box would see to that, heal her good as new.

'Mine's blackberry. Picked fresh from the bush.' Zander noisily sucked the dregs from his palate, tongue slapping. 'Ah, that's good. The best thing I've tasted since that last suds of McMud's, back on the old place.'

Kubla remembered. While she'd eaten her last Earth meal – her special request, strawberries dusted with crystalline lavender sugar – Zander had stood, boots apart, and leaning back, to neck down a jet black bottle of – she'd noticed as he cast it aside with a clatter – something unlabelled, without a single indicator to its contents.

'McMud's,' was the whole of his reply, when she'd asked him about it.

He'd been reticent, challenged by nerves maybe, in the pre-flight prep room, in final launch isolation, the few hours dragging by before their entry into Space Lab, and blast off.

Gosh, she felt homesick now. For a bowl of strawberries. A stack of green beans on a proper plate. For other *people*. For a sip of ... McMud's, even.

She relaxed into the back of her armchair. The sleep draught was taking effect. *Mmmm*, she thought. *That's better.*

'Did you hear what I said, when you came in?' from Zander, being careful.

'That you don't like it when things don't go your way,' she recalled, nodding. 'Coulda tole' you that.'

'I *said*, I'm not good when things don't go *right*,' Zander repeated, edging to the front of his seat.

'Same diff'rence,' she said.

'I ... suppose,' he conceded. She saw something in his face. Frustration? Something he was finding hard to say, or not say?

'When you puked,' he began, 'back on our first go down, in Big Lander ... the thing is, it shouldn't have happened.'

'Accidents happen in the best regulated families,' she said rapidly, one of her fave sayings tripping off her numbed tongue. 'And it was your fault anyway, giving me that frothy cap like you went and did.'

'I know. *I know*. But when things don't happen the way they should happen ... I find it ... hard to get over. I'm not good with those type of things.'

That phrase again. *I'm not good.* No, he wasn't.

'You're bad,' she said, waving a hand as if to flick at a fly that never existed. She pointed her finger straight at him: 'You. Put rats. On me. And Wanda.'

'I – ' he paused. Was he going to deny it? 'No you're right, I did that,' he said, sinking into his own chair, his eyes looking into hers, all puppy sad, but a puppy you couldn't trust wouldn't still steal your chocolate next chance it got. 'That was all me,' he said evenly. 'And I'm sorry.'

She nodded. She was definitely woozy. So was he, by the sound of things.

'So you give me a frothy cap and I puke it down your neck and you're Mr McGrump forever since when?'

He sighed. 'It takes me time to ... get over things.'

He turned his head down and to the side, more doggie behaviour. What for this time? Had he chewed one of her socks? Piddled on the floor? Or was it still just the same guilt because he'd put a rat on someone and stood by and watched?

Kubla creased her brows. She was pretty one hunnerd percent certain he hated her ... so what was this all about? Now, of all times, when they were sleepy? She decided to probe.

'So why'd you not dump me. And Alphy, and Beattie, and go off with the A Team there, Weezly and, and Wanda Woman?'

'*Veezl* and *Vonda*,' he corrected her, with

amusement. Actually smiling now. Generously. And was he *pleased* with her? That was new.

But had she misheard *Wanda* all along? Her mind wobbled. *Had* she?

'The Two V's,' Zander said.

She frowned, almost laughed, wasn't sure, then did anyway. 'Sometimes I find your humour ...' Something.

'I wasn't joking,' he said, 'not entirely.' He massaged the creases of his mouth with thumb and forefinger before saying, 'That's what everyone called them at Star Academy.'

Kubla: 'You *knew* them?'

'Sure.'

'They knew *you*?'

'Ditts.'

She was drowning in her armchair. She righted herself with her elbows, and struggled up for gulps of Space Lab air. Her mother used to say that open mouths caught bad apples, but Kubla wasn't able to close hers – she was gobsmacked.

'And it's not Wanda – it's *Vonda*?'

He nodded. 'It was, back when. She's changed it, somewhere along the line.'

'And you *know* her.' Her eyes standing out on stalks

a little, Zander seeming to shrink under her suddenly wide-awake gaze.

'Look,' he said, in retreat, 'I'll give you the whole once-upon-a-time, if you need it. I was ... going to anyway.'

So that was it. She watched him draw his knees up protectively. He strained forwards and put the empty paper cup on the coffee table, then sat back again slowly, his eyes once again meeting hers softly, with a gentleness.

'I knew Vonda Dace when she had an overbite that could have felled redwoods.' His eyes searched the heavens, and came back. 'She was in my school year.'

Kubla's sucked a breath in through her open mouth. This was *amaze*.

'Kind of lived next door, too,' Zander continued, curling one corner of his mouth upwards, and then downwards. 'I mean, she was right there. Unavoidable.'

'You two were –' her mouth moving as if forming his words for him.

'Girlfriend and boyfriend. For *at least* 24 hours. Took her to the Junior Prom. And all the usual shattering of impending joyous reality. In others words, she left me in the parking lot.'

'Oh, my –'

'And that was that. She just liked older boys. With cars. Sporting facial hair. The boyfs, not the cars,' he added, with a little snuckle that made her like him for a moment.

'Oh, you poor –'

'So I followed her through high school, helped with her homework, waited for her light to wink out at night before I slept, followed her to *Star* School.' He spread his palms – *there, now you know me.*

'You *stalked* her?' Warily.

'Nah, nothing like that. Just chose the same place to study. The same classes, too, mostly. Not stalking as such ... ' he paused musingly, as if he'd never considered until now that he might have crossed a line. 'Or maybe did I?'

He whistled through his teeth, seeming a gazillion miles away. Took a while to return to planet Space Lab. 'So she dated one hairball after another,' he reported, 'all the while gravitating towards the biggest wosspot on site ... well, you've met him.'

His gaze prompted her to say, 'Weasel?'

'Indeed.'

There was room to elaborate, but neither felt the need. To have met the Amagoo One Commander even briefly was to know him completely.

'The Two V's,' Kubla said, wanting to try out the words. 'Vonda, and Veezl.'

And she very, very slowly raised flat palms, the fingers pointing skywards before she parted them, Spockily, from many hours of juvenile practice, into two pairs, thumbs tucked in. And had the pure pleasure of seeing Zander P. Drum spontaneously erupt with a huge 'HA!', and continue HA-ing, his face glowing.

When he'd finished, she asked, 'And what happened after Star School? Did you keep in touch?'

'Oh, they deckered off to private enterprise. Didn't even take an exam, moved on from Star School before the end of second year. Go straight to Amagoo, Do Not Pass Go.'

'And you ... finished your studies and joined Space Lab?'

'Nah. Left right after they did, and signed up for the Foreign Legion!'

At which point the two space adventurers were left rolling in their armchairs, tears running down their faces, heads rocking from side to side, stomachs aching. Kubla had ejected a sip of her nighty-night drink onto her chin. She worked it back into her mouth with the side of her finger as she recovered her breath. She'd never laughed like that. Not with anyone.

'And then, after the ...' she hesitated, 'I can't say it or I'll be off again ...' while he stared at the heavens, his mouth a broad rictus grin.

'I did my year,' he said then, back in the room with her. 'In the Foreign.' He pulled up the short sleeve of his T-shirt to show her the top of his left arm. An emblem was tattooed there.

'Daffy Duck?'

'It's non-official,' he explained, and left his explanation there. 'After the Legion I came home. Did some currency dealing, played some poker ... some time inside ...'

'No! In prison?'

Rubbing his nose, nodding. 'And that's where that whatshername of yours found me.'

They both knew. 'J.P. Klaff. Co-Chair of the Consortium for the Choosing of Space Explorers.'

'That her. The Astrologist.'

'She said you had the highest IQ in the world.' And when he didn't respond. 'Did you ... cheat the test?'

'Nah.'

A little surprised, Kubla hurriedly disguised it with, 'You must have ... worked so hard through school?'

'Nah.'

She thought he seemed embarrassed. For being so

clever, so easily. And so he should be – it was hateful that he didn't have to try, the way she had done. Yet another reason to hate him. Though at this point she was mainly feeling sorry for him.

In fact – the thought flit across her mind – if it hadn't been for the Rat Incident, she'd have been feeling *fully* sorry for him. But that, with the rat ... was too ... raw a thing. It needed ... responding to ... a response ... to equal things up, before she could file it away and forget about it forever. In any case, all was in place. For that.

Kubla said, to fill the silence between them, 'Let me do a bedtime story, before we go to our boxes.'

And Zander, darting a look of surprise at her, gave her a definite thumb's up.

chapter
twenty-four

'IT'S CALLED *The Earth Mouse and the Space Mouse*,' Kubla said, with a winning smile.

'You sure 'bout that?' Negativity from Zander. 'I mean, you have, I hope, duly considered its appropriateness and general sleep-inducingness. With us being out here and a long way from home ... we don't want to have nightmares now, do we?'

'Don't be so grumpy,' Kubla chided. 'My Granpa used to tell me this story – *all* the time. And I loved it.'

'Then I suppose we'd better hear it.' Zander making a show of settling himself, and nestling his grizzled cheek on the fingers of his closed right hand.

'Okay, if you are sitting comfortably? I shall begin.'
And Kubla's mind was blank.

'Hang on,' she said, pouting hard.

'I'm, as you say, hanging,' Zander said, dry as a bone that'd never met drool. Then, 'Soz, I meant, take your time, there's no hurry.'

'How did it go now?' Her brain woozed. Parts of it wanted to sleep already, other parts to entertain, and be entertaining. She was ... multitudinous, that was the word. Now this story, how the Dickens did it begin?

'I'm guessing,' Zander offered, as if reading her mind, 'that a thing *upon* a something might get us started. Maybe, I'm thinking, Once Upon a Planet Earth there was ...'

'A Mouse!' And she had it, coming suddenly to life like her childhood music box: a ballerina sprang up, and the music began.

'Do go on.'

'And it lived on Earth. The Mouse.' She cleared her throat and started over. 'Once Upon a ... Planet Earth, yes, that's good ... there was a Mouse, and it lived on Earth, and it was happy there.'

'Where?'

'London! No! Shanghai! No! San Francisco! One of those tenements, with a basement.'

'Little fella lived in the basement.' Zander sounding satisfied. 'Not far off Market. He'd never got himself down to Pier 39, but this fine rodentious fellow didn't give a squeak.'

Kubla nodded. 'It did not,' she agreed, pleased. And why not be pleased? Zander was enjoying himself. And so was she. Why shouldn't she let her mission partner get in on the story too? It would be like pairs of friends at school she'd seen, often imagined herself part of, who'd shared good times so enjoyably.

'That's right,' she said, inclusively. 'What you said. And a jolly good Earth life it had.'

'He had.'

'Or She.'

'Definitely He.'

'Well, I think you're wrong, Zander my dear, I think. Our Mouse is a She, I really think it so.'

'Living alone in that neighbourhood?'

Kubla considered. Imagined streets cast stark in the shadow of skyscrapers, brutal qualities of light; a city area with a good reputation, yet susceptible to the sirens of police and ambulance, the dead bang of a gun.

She had to concede. In any case, she'd hardly got the story going, didn't want it to crash and burn so soon.

'O-kay,' she said, and enjoying her new thought even before she said it: 'He *and* she – two mice! Eh? Eh?'

He regarded her from beneath his eyebrows. Nodded sagely, approvingly. Then, 'So to recaperoo, there were these *two* squeakers living on Earth, and happy as can be.' Zander held his hands interlaced in his lap, then tucked loose fists under his chin. 'What happens next?'

'And each day,' she said quickly, 'was a good day, with plenty to do, and plenty to eat, and plenty to watch on TV!'

She watched Zander's thumb slip into his mouth, and felt a warmth somewhere bellywards. For him? Absolutely not. Well, yes and no, or maybe. For his child-like attention to this story, possibly.

'And at night they slept under the stars,' she said by way of moving quickly on.

Zander gave her a double take. 'In the *basement?*' he wondered, around his thumb.

'When it was warm, they'd trek from their tiny basement to the rooftop balcony, dragging cute little sleeping bags and pillows behind them.'

A slow, affirmative blink from Zander.

'And there, one night,' Kubla continued, more fluidly, 'they talked of their cousin – no, cousin*s* – who lived in Space, and roundabouts Stars and Galaxies.'

She paused to let Zander interject, but he remained

silent. She wondered if she'd ever seen him so still before.

Kubla was sure she had not.

'It so happened,' she continued, 'that their cousins, the Space Mice, came to visit. And what a time they had! All around the neighbourhood they went, and further afield, into growing fields even, where they picked, or nibbled rather, corn off the stems, and sipped fresh water from those deep mineral springs you get.'

Kubla's thoughts drifted. She'd seen and even drank from a freshwater spring like that once. As a child. And on the same day, watched a geyser that shot white spume into the sky every hour. With her mother, that was. Such a very long time ago.

'And all was good,' she said, 'and warm, and right.'

Because it had been, for one weekend out of her childhood.

'After that,' Kubla explained, 'the cousins from the stars were keen for the Earth mice to visit them next, the place they lived, in Space, on a spaceship, where their every need was taken care of.'

Zander's head began to lower. If he fell asleep here she might have to get him into his suspended animation box. Which wouldn't be right, she liked to be first to sleep, to go under while there was still someone about. In case of ... well, in case of something.

Kubla felt her eyelids sliding over gritty surfaces, her thoughts drifting to her own box, which she'd already made up, her pillow plumped in readiness and waiting, the twin of her regular bunkbed; though somehow her box was even more comfortable, perhaps because of the eternally long, dream-filled sleep it offered.

She sighed sleepily, then shook herself more awake, and with one foot kicked the other, a method of revival she'd learned sitting at her desk in hot classrooms.

It was the nighty-night drink. Just that. Making her lose it.

'So out to Outer Space they went,' she said, with effort, as Zander slipped from his paisley armchair, slow as treacle, to pudding on the floor, the oversized T-shirt giving the look of a dusty dark-chocolate coating, with a head.

'And out there in Outer Space,' Kubla continued, half-drunk, 'life was so different – and so very *easy*. Around the ship the cousins – the four of 'em – the pair of pairs, heehee – sauntered, sampling from vending units a galaxy of foods and tastes, all the while feeling like the first mice, the true mice, the top-of-the-class mice ...'

'Did a cat get 'em?' Zander's dark raisin eye watching her.

'Something,' she admitted, 'did. A robot, or a cat. Or an alien, or space bug. *Tried* to get them, for sure. Scared the bejulips out of the Earth guys. So they suited, the He and the She, and got home again, and fast.'

Kubla felt chill. Zander had been right. It was the wrong story to tell.

'They really get home again? They were happy, again?' Zander slowly pushing himself up. 'What's the point in that story?'

Was there a tear in his eye?

'Is this really about mice?' he said, in earnest; then, emotionally, 'What a piece of capo!'

Kubla might easily have slept where she sat. She dragged her head up. Zander, who had attained an upright posture on wobbly legs, was with his sleep-zombie body and loose arms attempting to beckon her.

'C'mon,' he croaked, 'we're stragglin' too long ... got to let heads hit the ...'

Drool hung from his chin. He dragged it across his forearm, looked dizzy for a count of three, then, 'Bedtimes, I'm sayin',' he sighed, and stumbled to the adjoining room, where their boxes awaited them.

Kubla tried to hurry, she had to be first, always was.

She made it just in time. Keyed in her code. Reclined and fidgeted.

'Thank you for my bedtime story!' she heard him call dutifully and with only the mildest sarcasm, as he clumsily arranged and then climbed into his box.

'No you're welcome!' she managed, feeling suddenly sure she'd gone too far, much too far, much too late too far, as her box lid closed, and the next moment that she'd never been happier than she was now, this the first day of her new dream job, taking albino unicorn bunnies for walks over rainbows, bathed in the sparkle of soft, glittery rain.

chapter
twenty-five

LYING ON HIS BACK, his body hand-in-glove with
the contours of his personal mattress, Zander watched
the lid of his box falling slowly towards his face,
eclipsing the room's blue glow until the last ethereal
edge winked out.

'Funky,' he said to only himself, groggily.

It wasn't dark in the box, for which he was grateful.
He actually didn't much mind the being-sealed-in-a-
tight-spot aspect of suspended animation, just so long
as the nightlight didn't go out. Something about having
a streetlamp outside his childhood bedroom, perhaps?
Or too many *Tales of the Unexpected* reruns, at a delicate
age?

The box's walls, floor and lid were non-transparent,

and so technically speaking it could have been as dark as doodoo inside, once the roof was down. There were, however, twin tracks of cheerfully orange runway lights – like carefully spaced soft-focus satsumas – running from either side of Zander's head and out of sight towards his feet.

'Nice,' was his comment, the first time he'd seen them.

He listened to air being discretely farted from the innards of high-spec, triple-flanged suction seals, followed by three long, low and sleepy electronic beeps to reassure him that he was now hermetically isolated from the world, the Universe, and the entirety of existence, including all cloned and born humans – Kubla's face ghosting across his mind – who were now all firmly *outside* his box.

Which was fine by him, Zander thought, his weight sinking more deeply into his mattress as his breathing began to draw out. The sleeping draught in his blackberry nighty-night was working to good effect. He was at ease, could relax bodily, neck to ankles, even those last tight little muscles around jaw and temples, along neck and shoulders, elbows and wrists.

A pleasurable sigh; a longer in-breath rounded off by an orgastic, piglike snuffle. Everything was good.

With Zander, his soul, and the safe and secure life-supporting space he now occupied. Run off and join the Foreign Legion? Forget it. Suspended animation ... now *that* was a vacation from the world's botherations. *Highly* recommended.

Finally, and at last, and with mucho welcome, all was well with Zander P. Drum.

Or was it? Some hangnail, some kind of loosed-shoelace sensation was surfing across the quieted surface of his mind, making ripples that ... persisted.

And yet it was evidently too late. For even as anxious thoughts began to germinate, his brain was dragged chemically back down into a dormant state, where seedling electrical stimulations bloomed only into wasteful dreams, and he found himself sitting on a park bench, lilacs everywhere, waiting for a tram to arrive along the grass, due any minute, himself hooded, all packed up and ready for the off, watching a bumblebee make a stop-and-turn, then with a sudden high-octane blaze from its rear end, buzz off straight to the heavens ...

And he was back in his box again, his eyes half open, heavy lidded, his mind grinding gears.

'Was it a rat I saw?' his lips mumbled, muffled by numbness.

He took a sharp breath.

A rat would be ... nasty.

And what he probably deserved.

But ... was it? Wasn't it? No, not a rat, or any other living thing — the box would have detected that. So it could be ... he listened intently, alertly.

Something was *ticking*.

Zander screwed up his face, in an effort to wring the suds from his brain.

About one tick per second. Clocklike. And that – his heart seemed to suck in a huge volume of blood, and then pause – was as scary as anything because nothing, not one single component, in a suspended animation box or even within Space Lab itself had a ticking clock. Because it just plain didn't need one and who on Dog's Earth world tolerate the ticking of ... Oh, my giddy aunt she got me!

Fumbling in the tight confines up and down the sides of his box, he soon located the thing, jammed under the rise in his thin mattress where his knees were supported, and where he'd surely be least likely to ever notice it.

He grasped it in his fist; drew it to his nose to examine.

Oh yes, she'd really got him - or nearly did. His

estimation of her elevating to Everest levels as he, in the dim orange light, examined Kubla's ages-old pink plastic alarm clock, wrapped in polythene. By the looks of it, the alarm primed to ring out its tinny wakeup call every twelve hours. Until its AA batteries ran down. This to cause him undoubted mental trauma during sleep, at the very least – and quite possibly a full wakeup from suspended animation due to systems designed to detect noise from within the box.

Which would require a minimum two weeks alone moping around Space Lab before initiating another hibernation.

Zander grinned, couldn't help himself. He hadn't thought she had it in her. Why, she had facets, that one! She had – something lively about her, more than you saw when you saw her.

He frown-smiled, enjoying himself. His shipmate was, had just magically become, a sparring partner worth her stripes. Someone to keep him on his toes. There would be fun to be had.

Distracted by such thoughts, Zander carelessly didn't bother analyzing why his practical-joking, revenge-dishing flight partner had sealed her pink alarm clock in an airtight plastic bag filched, against regulations, from a sample collection kit.

'Tsk, tsk,' he tsked, 'going rebel, too, are you? There's hope for you yet.'

He tore the bag in two with his fingernails. Immediately wished he hadn't.

The stench raked upwards through his sinuses, attacking his frontal lobe, bursting against the walls of his eyeballs, stabbing on eardrums; white-hot needles penetrated to his feet and back up inside legs to pincushion into his crotch and inner organs. By the time he'd emitted his first yell of horror, the stink was bellowed from his lungs into the air around him, ready and primed for another go round.

Zander later believed his mind had been temporarily unhitched, was not still within him, only returning to its post towards the tail end of a period of yelling, kicking and screaming; screams that, his returning consciousness noticed, were somehow harmonizing with a startled beeping from his box, both sounds slowly fading until they'd stopped altogether, but not quite stopped, dispersed more like, out into space possibly, hopefully never to return.

Leaving just him, his satsumas, and the reek.

He thought clearly: she's gotten a chunk of nose-turd in here with me. The alarm clock was a ruse, only a decoy, to draw attention, and to cloud his reasoning.

Making sure he'd open the bag. The portion of nose-turd surely located by stealth inside the body of the alarm clock itself.

Genius.

Zander, self-preservation kicking in, made himself listen and think.

His box was functioning.

He listened again.

The ticking had stopped.

He listened again — and heard nothing disturbing.

There was a hunk of moon turd in here with him for the next 12400.5 days – somewhere down by his feet, where in his panic he'd spontaneously launched the torn airlock bag, alarm clock, spilled batteries and all – but otherwise, everything was just ... stinky dinky.

Hastily, before sleep sedated him, he considered his options. Air refresh buttons were not fitted. These hibernation caves were far too fancy for something so crude, their main concern being delicate air composition, as in oxygen-carbon dioxide balance. The idea being to adjust the atmosphere only mildly, keep things subtle and steady.

He had but two choices.

Abort suspended animation, set it all up again, and

endure the two weeks of prep. (In other words, be by himself for a fortnight.)

Or just sleep with it.

He was so tired … as she'd have known he would be.

A small smile raised the edge of his mouth.

He would do nothing, only sleep and give in to his fate, accept his punishment, in all likelihood fully deserved. He would marinate in nose-worm stink, the very flavour of which was already making him think for some reason not of revenge, but of their B3POBOX77 adventure, and the way she'd single-mindedly bounded across the moon surface to scramble back into Big Lander, before he maybe took off and left her. Such memory coupled with a strange, squeezy feeling about his ribs hitherto only experienced on watching the birth of puppies.

Zander snuckered up a snore.

He was just so damned proud of her, was all the reason for that rare left-chestal sensation, he told himself

…

and was gone.

Addendum:

THE NEOCRETE SPONGE

Type of thing: Uphe
    Category: Major

The Neocrete Sponge has unrivalled celebratory status due to its dual characteristics of being both the most geographically ubiquitous of late 21st Century *Uphes*, and yet the least known about in detail.

Originally the concept of Japanese grot artist Ichinose X, The Neocrete Sponge was devised as a minute spongiform animalcule said to inhabit solely the cracks in white concrete in the Fdfdfd district of Tokyo; between three and four metres above sea level; with four centimetres penetration.

Never seen by the naked eye, or even by a fully clothed technician wielding an electron microscopette, and, in fact, known from the outset to never have existed at all, being completely made up in the Ichinose X braincules, The Neocrete Sponge uphe flashed across the planet in minutes, took permanent residence in the minds of most of its inhabitants, and remained there, to all intents and purposes forgotten, except for when called upon by those deficient in, and in need of, extra vocabulary.

Examples in *common* usage include,

What the Dickens! You're about as useless as The Neocrete Sponge!

No reception here either, Kevin ... we're lost like The Neocrete Sponge ... I give up!

If only we had The Neocrete Sponge here, Inspector Dufus, my alibi would be watertight.

And so on, and so on. And so on.

Usage in popular literature worldwide, according to AG search engine, numbers 14, 120, 567, 9000001245 and 7.

about the author

Sam Keck is the author of this book.
They have never been to Barnsley.

books by sam keck

Space Lab Book One: War of the Noses